"Timothy?" she called, hoping he was here somewhere, maybe just hidden by the roiling clouds of fog. "Where are you?"

A full minute passed, maybe more, before he answered. "Back here, Paige," he said, sounding strangely distant. "In the trees."

She looked to where the sound of his voice had come from—a thick growth of trees across the grassy patch and flower beds from the windmill. Staring through the mist between the trees, she finally spotted a pale oval she thought must be Timothy's face.

"What are you doing in there?" she asked with a nervous chuckle. "Come on out here."

"It's safer in the trees," Timothy replied.

"Safer?" Paige echoed. "Safe from what?"

MIRROR IMAGE

Charmed®

Published by Simon & Schuster

MIRROR IMAGE

An original novel by Jeff Mariotte

Based on the hit TV series created by

Constance M. Burge

SIMON SPOTLIGHT ENTERTAINMENT
New York   London   Toronto   Sydney

This book is a work of fiction. Any references to historical events, real people, or real locales are used fictitiously. Other names, characters, places, and incidents are the product of the author's imagination, and any resemblance to actual events or locales or persons, living or dead, is entirely coincidental.

First Simon Spotlight Entertainment edition April 2004
First Simon Pulse edition July 2003

S|S|E

SIMON SPOTLIGHT ENTERTAINMENT
An imprint of Simon & Schuster
Children's Publishing Division
1230 Avenue of the Americas
New York, NY 10020

SIMON SPOTLIGHT ENTERTAINMENT and related logo are
trademarks of Simon & Schuster, Inc.

The text of this book was set in Palatino.

Manufactured in the United States of America

10 9 8 7

Library of Congress Control Number 2002117610
ISBN-13: 978-0-689-85790-4
ISBN-10: 0-689-85790-X

MIRROR IMAGE

Prologue

The San Francisco fog, furious clouds of it that blotted out the sky, the hills, and even the tops of the buildings across the street, had rolled in thick and fast that afternoon. Julia Tilton, running a little late for work, had felt the dampness of the early evening on the streetcar and now, pushing up the steep hill of Polk Street, had to battle to convince herself that it was only the angle of ascent, not the fog itself creating some kind of solid barrier against her, that made the going difficult. By the time she made it to work her shoulder-length blond hair would be totally plastered to her head, and as it dried, frizz city.

She knew La Terraza wouldn't go bankrupt if she was ten minutes late for work. Jeannie would stay on a little longer, and as soon as Julia got there, she'd throw on her apron and take over her own tables. No big. There were only fourteen tables anyway, and Jeannie had covered dinners solo before. But Mr. Marzolla got so agitated, his face turning red except for that one patch on his balding forehead that stayed so white it looked like some kind of blooming carnation against a crimson background, that it was frightening, if a little comical at the same time. He'd haul her into the cramped kitchen and rant and scream as if she'd hacked his bank account and drained every penny out of it.

Lou Marzolla's temper was the primary reason Julie scanned the *Chronicle* each morning looking for a new job. But she liked the people she worked with, her boss notwithstanding, and the schedule was pretty flexible, and they had a lobster sauce to die for. And she'd waited on three movie stars since she had started there, two years before. Okay, Shawn Cassidy was more of a TV star, she guessed, and maybe a little past his prime, but Susan Sarandon was legitimately a movie star, and Clint Eastwood—well, he was Clint Eastwood! He had a face that wouldn't have been out of place on Mount Rushmore, and he'd been just as nice as could be. A big tipper, too. That never hurt a bit.

So the job search continued, but slowly, as each possibility Julia examined fell short in one way or another. Her house search had gone better. She'd had to move a month ago, when her apartment building had gone condo, but she'd found a place with three roommates, an airy second-story walk-up in the Mission District. The place was a little run-down, but affordable for the four of them. Inspired by that success, she'd come to see the morning paper as her salvation and scoured it daily for that perfect job, recognizing, even as she did, that a perfect job might not exist.

The urgency to find out would come much sooner if she didn't get to the restaurant before Mr. Marzolla blew a fuse. But the fog threw off her senses, made her feel as if she were hardly making any progress up the hill at all. It also seemed to alter sound, dampening it somehow, making her feel as if she were alone in the city. The street was mostly empty. The sun had set while she walked; a few cars flashed by on Pine, up the hill, their headlights cutting through the soup and their tires shushing on wet pavement, but here on Polk all she could hear were her own breathing and footfalls on the concrete.

At least, that was all she *thought* she could hear at first.

As she climbed, though, she realized that the ragged breathing she could hear wasn't only her own. Someone else was nearby, matching breaths with her. She intentionally altered her rhythm and heard a sharp inhalation that cut off suddenly.

Julia stopped and spun around on the street.

There was no one in sight, just fog, drifting in thick patches across the empty block. But she could have sworn she'd heard someone. . . .

Maybe just the fog playing tricks on me, she guessed. *Bouncing sounds around and echoing, throwing me off.* She tried to push her worries out of her mind and started up the hill again, but after a few steps she stopped short and held her breath again.

Then she heard it once more, a footfall that landed slightly after hers and a quickly abbreviated exhalation. She felt a—a *presence*, she thought, as if someone were right there with her. She didn't like the feeling at all.

"Who's there?" she asked, whirling around again. Still no one. Was she cracking up? Maybe there wasn't enough oxygen getting to her brain.

She turned back up the hill once more. Not much farther to go. A few blocks, and she'd be at the little restaurant. A fire would be crackling in the fireplace, and Marzolla would be glaring at her, Jeannie giving her an understanding smile. She'd be safe soon. She took a step and then felt something soft and moist, like a wet strand of spiderweb, brush her cheek. She let out a sharp squeal and slapped at thin air.

"What is that?" she demanded of no one in particular. "Who's there?" No one answered, but before she could take another step, she felt another wet touch, this one on her neck. She slapped at it again but once again struck nothing.

This whole thing is impossible, she decided. *There's nothing here. It's just the damp, the fog. I'm sweating from the hurry and the steep hill, and it's trickling down my face and neck. That's all it is. Get a grip, girl.*

She had almost convinced herself when a voice spoke up, a voice that was soft and tentative and definitely male. "So pretty," the voice said.

That's when Julia Tilton screamed and started to run.

Her mistake was that she ran in the wrong direction—uphill, the way she had been heading, instead of down, where she might have been able to build up some real speed.

This is not happening, she thought. *This is so not happening. There isn't anything that has not happened that has been more not happening than this.*

But she had barely gone six steps up the steep hillside when she felt another touch, this one most decidedly not gentle: a shove, right at the small of her back, that drove her to her knees. She felt the sidewalk rip her black cotton pants, tear skin off her kneecaps, and she remembered briefly how, when she'd been ten and eleven, she'd gone through a real tomboy phase and had spent two glorious summers with perpetually skinned knees and raw palms from climbing and running and falling down so much.

There was no time for reminiscing now, though. She swung her purse wildly at whoever was back there, not connecting with anything. She choked down a sob, felt tears trailing her cheeks, and forced herself to her feet. Still no one there that she could see, but she knew somehow that it didn't matter if she could see him. He was there, and he meant her no good. She let out a scream, then, a real good one, long and loud and tinged with panic.

He just laughed and closed a powerful hand upon her shoulder. She lashed out again, this time making contact, but as soon as she did, when her hand touched something that almost felt like flesh, it simply went away, and her hand passed through the area that had been solid a split second before. For a brief moment she thought she saw a male face grinning at her through the mist, but then it was gone, and she couldn't be sure that it had ever been there at all.

This is a bad dream, she thought, *a nightmare because this can't be real. The world doesn't work this way. Something is solid or it's not, it has form and definition or it doesn't, it doesn't shift and change like the fog, and . . .*

And then Julia Tilton had no more even semi-coherent thoughts. Panic, real panic that slashed consciousness to ribbons, took over. She began to sob and moan and utter short gasps that almost sounded like barks, her tears were a river, the mighty Mississippi cutting down her face, and she trembled like an aspen leaf in a stiff Sierra wind. It was a terrible moment for her, but brief, and maybe merciful in a way, because when the long knife flashed in a stray beam of sunlight that cut through the fog, her mind had already left her and the fear wasn't as awful as it would have been even a few moments before.

Chapter

1

Every house makes noise at night; older ones just make more of it, with causes both obvious and obscure. Sharing an old Victorian with two sisters, Paige Matthews thought, meant that strange sounds were virtually guaranteed. She supposed her sisters had to put up with her weirdnesses too. But then, it wasn't as if they hadn't had to cope with a sister before her—Prue, who had died not so long ago, had lived with them in the same house until her untimely death. So in a way, she guessed, her presence in the house was probably more comforting than distracting, a way of returning the house to its normal state.

Normal, in the sense of crowded and chaotic, that was.

The house wasn't small, but any house that contained three headstrong sisters—and two significant others—within its walls, Paige was convinced, was bound to feel claustrophobic from time to time. And she had no illusions that she wasn't every bit as headstrong as the others. Maybe a little more so sometimes.

As Paige brushed her luxurious dark hair—a hundred strokes, every night before bed when she wasn't out fighting demons or rescuing innocents from some unworldly evil—she heard high-pitched laughter that she believed emanated from Phoebe's room. That meant Cole was here. Phoebe always laughed like that—in a good way—when he was around. In most households, coming and going were easier to keep track of because people used these handy inventions called doors, but in this one folks were constantly orbing in and out, appearing and vanishing, often without notice.

Sometimes listening to them set her teeth on edge, and then that made her feel disloyal and ungrateful. She wasn't—not in the least. They were her sisters, though she had learned about them only recently, after Prue's death. The discovery that the mom who had left her to be adopted had borne three other daughters paled in comparison to the fact that their mom had been a witch, and Paige's dad—though not the father of Piper and Phoebe—had been a Whitelighter. But Phoebe and Piper had accepted Paige into the family, taken her into the ancestral manor, taught her about her witchy heritage, and treated her like the sister she was. She couldn't begrudge them a thing.

No, she thought maybe it had more to do with the fact that they were just so darn *happy* with the respective men in their lives. Paige liked men—maybe a little too much sometimes, which had led to trouble once or twice. But now that she was a witch, her options seemed to have become very limited. Normal human guys didn't really fit the new lifestyle. They were at risk from all sorts of badness, and she had discovered that most didn't tend to react too well to the revelation that she and her sisters had supernatural powers. Piper had already sewn up their Whitelighter, so Paige couldn't pull a repeat of their mom's trick. Phoebe had Cole, an ex-demon, and that sometimes worried Paige because she wasn't sure just how *ex* an ex-demon could really be, and witches and demons were more or less the dogs and cats of the magical world.

So whom did that leave available for Paige? No Whitelighter, no handy former demons turned good, no humans around who seemed totally comfortable with the whole deal. Maybe somewhere there was a hot male witch who didn't happen to be a relative, but if there was, she hadn't met him yet.

She put down the brush and ran through her mental going-to-bed checklist. Hair, teeth, face. Outfit for tomorrow chosen, but left in the closet, where it was safer from any gooey evil types that might decide to invade the house during the night. She had said her goodnights. Done then. She peeled off her fluffy cotton robe, tossed it over the back of a chair, and slid between her sheets. Paige loved clean sheets, all crisp and cool, and while she would never claim to be the neatest housekeeper in the world—or even in the house—she did try to change her bed as often as possible.

As she rested her head on the pillow, she realized what it was that bothered her about her sisters sometimes. It wasn't anything they did. It was nothing more than pure envy. She wanted what they had: relatively stable relationships with men who knew their secret and accepted them anyway. Appreciated them even. But she didn't know how to go about getting that, and she knew, realistically, that she should be happy with what she did have: two terrific sisters who cared about her, a roof over her head, and a purpose in life. There were plenty of people with far, far less than that.

Paige closed her eyes and within a few minutes had drifted off to sleep.

Fog lay over the city like a shroud, settling into every cranny it could find, muffling light and sound and smell. From the Golden Gate to Hunter's Point, from the tourist traps along the Embarcadero to the silent shoreline of Lake

Merced, San Francisco drowsed under the cool, damp layer.

The precise origins of Halliwell Manor were lost to history, but as far as anyone knew, the Victorian house had always been in the family. It had been built for San Francisco, meaning with fog and earthquakes in mind, and it had been restored and repaired many times, since enemies had long made a habit of bringing the battle of good versus evil to the witches who occupied it. All these things meant that with the windows closed as they were on this cold night, there was no easy entry point into the manor.

But the fog was nothing if not tenacious.

It tested; it prodded; it poked. Doorknobs, windows, shingles: All around the house, the fog sent tendrils snaking about, exploring for a way in. Finally, it found one, through a tiny hole beneath the eaves that had been missed in repairing the much larger hole a G'nesht Demon had made with a badly thrown fireball five months before.

Entry made, the tendril of fog wafted silently through the house, past the sleeping occupants, finally pausing over one of them. Then the finger of fog seemed to shake, and a puff of glittering nothingness dropped down on the sleeper's face, sparking out of existence the moment it brushed her skin.

One down. The fog moved on then, leaving that sleeper behind, not quite rousing from her sleep but wiping at her cheek as if to dry a spot of dampness. The ever-growing tentacle of fog, never breaking from the mass outside, went into another room, and repeated the same procedure. Again, a fine, almost nonexistent spray of twinkling light descended on a sleeping sister, who never woke but merely twitched her nose once and turned over.

Finally, the fog settled over the third sister, asleep alone in her room, and once more, it dusted a sleeper with something just this side of nothing at all. This third sister didn't react in the slightest.

The fog dissipated then, leaving behind only the faintest traces of moisture on the house's ceiling, which would dry well before morning.

No matter. Its work was done.

And the three sisters would never be the same. . . .

Phoebe had been sleeping soundly, without dreaming, barely aware of the handsome, dark-haired man who held her as he slumbered beside her. Without warning, she fell into a dream as if into a dark and terrifying chasm. The landscape was sharp-edged and scorched, the mood ominous. She could hear a distant wailing, sounding like the cries of the doomed, mothers who had lost their children, souls in eternal torment. She walked through this place and felt a chill that cut her to the bone.

Then, through dream logic, she was suddenly in a different place, inside Halliwell Manor, or more precisely, in the manor's attic. She noticed a dresser pushed up against a wall, one of those pieces of furniture that do nothing but collect dust, so omnipresent that one barely notices their existence. But if she had never noticed it before, she noticed it now. It almost thrummed with malice, giving off the same sort of emanation as the darkly terrifying place she had just left. As she watched the chest, seemingly observing it from every direction at once, her dream self not limited to mortal ways of seeing, it began to tremble, like something alive and terrified. All at once the drawers opened themselves, and blood, thick and crimson, with that familiar metallic tang, gushed out, splashing onto the old hardwood floor.

Phoebe sat up, instantly wide awake. She blinked a couple of times as the dream's reality faded from view, like the image of a camera's flash after a picture is snapped, then shook Cole until he stirred.

"What?" he mumbled. "What's wrong, Phoebe?"

"Cole, we have to go upstairs."

"Now?" he asked groggily. "It's . . . what time is it? Late. It's late. Or early."

"Now," Phoebe said. "Right now. Come on. Or don't, I don't care. I'll go alone."

This threat spurred him to greater effort. He sat

up and pushed the covers back. "No, okay. I'll come, Phoebe. Just hold on a second. What is it?"

"I had a vision," she told him. "Or not a vision, I guess, but a dream. A dream that was like a vision, kind of."

"In what way?" he asked, turning his legs and putting his bare feet on the floor. He looked awake now, and concerned, his adorable brow all ruffled the way it got when he was worried. She would have admired it more, but the dream/vision still had her pretty creeped out. "You don't have precognitive dreams, Phoebe. Like a vision how? What did you see?"

"It wasn't really a vision, I'm sure, just a really creepy dream. And not in the sense that I don't think I saw something that's actually going to happen. It wasn't precognitive. More, I don't know, symbolic, I guess. But like a vision in the sense that I feel that it's important, urgent, that people's lives could be in danger."

"Whose?"

"I have no idea," she said. She knew she was being very vague, but she knew only what she knew, and right now that wasn't much at all. "But someone's. I can't really tell you why. Maybe it's because of all the blood."

"Blood?" Cole echoed, concern furrowing his brow once again.

Phoebe wouldn't be swayed from her task. "Let's go upstairs."

It took a few minutes to find—the Halliwell

attic was not the most organized room of the Manor, and the detritus of generations of Halliwells was piled in front of the dresser—but it was there, as Phoebe had half remembered, and it looked, minus the trembling and all the fountaining blood, just the way it had in her dream. Blond wood, scuffed and stained with years of use, the knobs a darker wood carved in a kind of floral pattern, with a delicate inlay of still another wood around the outer perimeter. It had been a lovely item once. Phoebe was a little surprised none of the sisters had claimed it for her own room. She wasn't about to, not after that dream, but it looked like a piece that Piper might enjoy having.

"Okay," Cole said after they'd cleared a path to it through the boxes and accumulated belongings. "Now what?"

"Well, in the dream it just kind of shook and then spit blood," she told him. "Like it had been to a really bad dentist."

"It's not doing either of those things now," he said. "Which I'm just fine with, I might add." He looked at her with an expression she knew well. "I love you," it said. There was a dash of "I will always take care of you" thrown in. "Maybe it really was just a dream, Phoebe."

I love you too, she thought back toward him. But what she said was, "I know a dream when I have one, Cole. I've been dreaming for years now. And this was no *normal* dream. Call it a nightmare, call it whatever you want, but normal dreams are patently unreal. This one—I keep coming back to comparing it to a vision. I can *feel* that it had some deeper meaning."

He shrugged. He wasn't one to argue when it was clear that there was no hope of winning. "Okay then. I guess we should take a closer look. It'd help if we knew what we were looking for"—he caught her sharp glance— "but that's not really absolutely necessary, is it?"

They started with the obvious places. They looked inside all the drawers, then pulled them out and checked their backs and undersides, tapping for hidden compartments or false bottoms. Then they examined the bureau's shell, inside and out, trying to peel back any layers of veneer that might hide unpleasant secrets. Finally, Cole helped Phoebe move the heavy dresser away from the wall. It was immediately evident, then, that the back panel had been tacked on with small finishing nails at some point after the bureau had been made; the wood was completely different, the finish less worn, and no nails had been used in the original cabinetry work.

"Well, this has to come off," Phoebe said with a degree of satisfaction.

"That's going to be noisy," Cole told her.

"Like there's anyone still asleep with all the racket you two have been making?"

Phoebe and Cole both whirled around to see

Piper and Leo standing behind them, watching. Piper, clad in a long cotton nightshirt, looked bleary-eyed and maybe a bit on the grouchy side. Leo, as usual, seemed bright and chipper. "Apparently the dead don't need a whole lot of sleep," Piper had once told Phoebe. She had sounded a bit resentful at the time possibly because she *did* need sleep and hadn't been getting it.

Kind of like now.

"Where's Paige?" Phoebe asked.

"Okay, I take it back," Piper said. She rubbed at her cheek as if something were tickling her. "The one sister who could probably sleep through a thermonuclear explosion is still sleeping. Nobody else, though. So since I'm guessing this is not an episode of *Trading Spaces*, would somebody like to tell me what's going on?"

"Phoebe had a dream—," Cole started to speak.

"More than just a dream," Phoebe interrupted. "A visionlike dream. Powerful."

"And you dreamed the attic wasn't enough of a mess so you had to come up and start rearranging? In the middle of the night?"

"I dreamed," Phoebe said, "that there was something wrong with this bureau. And there is. Now we just need to get this back piece off and maybe we can find out what it is."

"Do you have a pry bar, Leo?" Cole asked. "Or even just a clawhammer?"

Before revealing himself to be the Charmed

Ones' Whitelighter, Leo's cover had been as the Manor's handyman. It had been, Phoebe often thought, a remarkably useful cover to have since there was just about always work to be done around the place.

"Sure," he said. "Just a minute."

Fortunately, he had stored his toolbox here in the attic when he married Piper and moved in for good. He disappeared behind some boxes and came back a moment later carrying a hammer and a flat chisel. "This should do it," he said. He joined Cole behind the bureau, and Phoebe stepped away to let the testosterone twins do their thing.

Two minutes later enough of the false panel had been peeled away to reveal an envelope stuffed between the bureau's real back and the panel. Phoebe snatched it up. "See?" she said, holding it up for Piper's benefit. "There *was* something here."

"Are you going to open it?" Piper inquired. "Or just assume it's bad news?"

She was probably right about that, Phoebe knew. A dream like the one she'd had just wouldn't be announcing happy news. But she had come this far, and she was already starting to open it. The envelope wasn't sealed, but its flap was tucked in. She slipped a finger behind the flap and peeled it back. Inside was a letter, written on a single sheet of age-browned paper, brittle with the passing of years. She scanned it quickly. "Can I say, 'I told you so' now, Piper? It *is* bad news," she muttered, going back to the start to read it over more thoroughly.

"What?" Piper demanded. "Come on, share."

"It's—it's from Aunt Agnes. Great-Aunt Agnes," Phoebe said.

"That would be great-great-great, I think," Piper corrected her. "At least."

Piper had always known the family tree better than Phoebe, so Phoebe let the correction stand. "Yeah, her," she said.

"And?"

"And it's a warning, it seems. It's addressed only to 'Charmed Ones.'"

"Well, that would be us. Warning about what?" Piper wanted to know.

"Here's the important part," Phoebe said. She started to read aloud. "'A sister shall die, and a new one shall take her place. But the new witch is no ally, mark me well. A traitor she is, and once entrusted by the family, this devil shall endanger the Power of Three. Let not this come to pass, lest ye be torn asunder from within the bosom of thine own family.'"

Piper was silent for a moment, absorbing the quote. "Yeah," she said after a minute. "And we're supposed to believe that? It sounds like it was written by a ten-year-old who heard too many ghost stories. Let's go back to bed, Leo."

"But . . ." Phoebe wasn't quite sure how to proceed, hating the direction her thoughts were leading her. "Maybe Aunt Agnes was a lousy writer. But you have to admit the scenario sounds a little familiar, right?"

"If you're thinking Paige, Phebes, I have to tell you, you're way off base." Piper sounded absolutely certain; Phoebe found that comforting. "Paige is our sister, our *real* sister, and that's all there is to it. She's no fraud, no devil come to tear us 'asunder.' If she were, the power of three wouldn't work anymore."

"It's a good point," Phoebe acknowledged grudgingly. "And I wish I could be as sure as you, Piper," Phoebe told her. "But I'm the one who had the dream, you know? I wouldn't have been led here unless there was some reason. And the sensation I got from the dream was of something truly evil. Even if Paige *is* Charmed, something might seriously be off in some other way."

"Well, maybe Great-Great-Great-Aunt Agnes was a little off her rocker," Piper suggested. "Maybe the dresser was made by an evil troll who happened to be good at woodshop. Who knows? All I know is, I know Paige, and she's not evil."

"I don't think she is either," Phoebe said. She was surprised at the vehemence of Piper's reaction. Normally, she believed her sister would at least *listen* to her point of view, be willing to entertain her ideas. But Piper was totally dismissing her, and she didn't like it one bit. The more Piper refused to consider Phoebe's theory, the more intransigent Phoebe felt about it. Rather than ask Piper what had gotten into her, she felt she didn't care to know. "I really don't. But I know what I felt, in the dream. And it wasn't good."

"Are you coming, Leo?" Piper asked coldly. She was already heading for the stairs. "I don't have the energy to argue about this and don't understand why anybody would waste their time even doubting Paige. She's proven herself to us."

"We all care about Paige," Cole put in. "But maybe you should pay a little attention to the sister you've known longer, Piper. She doesn't have any reason to want to hurt Paige. She's just looking at the facts in front of us."

"There *aren't* any facts," Leo said. "There's a letter that's probably a hundred years old. There's not a single indication that it's about Paige."

"I'm just saying we need to keep open minds," Cole replied. "Until we know for sure."

"I'm just saying that if I don't get back to bed, nobody's going to be happy," Piper said. "And I, for one, don't intend to spend another second doubting Paige's loyalty to this family." She turned and descended the staircase. Leo paused for a moment, looking back at Phoebe and Cole, then shrugged and followed her.

"Leo's right about one thing," Cole said. "We don't have any way of knowing what this letter applies to, if in fact it's a real warning."

"Except that we *are* the Charmed Ones. And I had a dream tonight," Phoebe told him. "I can't ignore my gut." Wearily she closed her eyes and set the letter on top of the bureau. "I don't want to suspect Paige of anything, Cole. I love her, you know that. But I know what I saw and what I felt."

Cole wrapped his arms around her, and she pressed herself into his comforting bulk. "Piper's right about one thing, though" he said quietly. "We should get back to sleep. We can figure out what to do in the morning."

"Yeah, I know," Phoebe replied. But she also knew that at least for this night, sleep would be hard to come by.

Chapter
2

Piper had awakened feeling as if she hadn't slept a wink. After Phoebe's little outburst in the attic, she had lain awake, listening to Leo snore—okay, not snore, exactly, but breathe louder than any human being had a right to, much less any human who had died half a century before and been sent back to earth to watch over witches—and staring into the dark. Phoebe was wrong about Paige. That fact was indisputable, and she felt an unexpected anger that Phoebe would even have considered it. *If Paige were some kind of spy or traitor,* she thought, *we would have figured it out by now.* She admitted she still didn't know Paige all that well—certainly not as well as she'd known Prue, who after all had been her older sister her whole life. *But she's not Mata Hari,* she thought.

A shower had helped, but not enough. Now, dressed in a soft green cotton top and jeans, Piper

24

sat at the table nursing a cup of coffee because actually lifting it and drinking deep required more energy than she could summon at this moment. It was starting to cool, and she debated the various merits of standing up and carrying it to the microwave to zap it, or zapping it herself, with a tiny, concentrated dose of her own witch power, speeding up the molecules enough to warm the tepid liquid. *Personal gain,* she thought, *a big witchy no-no,* so she settled for the relatively old-fashioned, but more labor-intensive, option.

Paige and Phoebe both were in the manor's cheerful yellow kitchen, Paige at the counter buttering half a toasted bagel and Phoebe ferociously stirring a glass pitcher of orange juice that she had just made from frozen concentrate. Piper thought about asking Phoebe if she was mad at the entire state of Florida or just its oranges, but bit back the words. She didn't exactly feel like joking around this morning. Especially with Paige in the room.

She and Phoebe both had been downstairs before Paige this morning and over a quick, hushed discussion had decided not to tell her anything about the events in the attic the night before, at least until they could check things out for themselves. Or Phoebe could check them out, since Piper didn't even want to dignify the letter by giving it a second thought.

It meant, of course, that it was all she *had* thought about.

Paige seemed to pick up on the tension in the room, though, and made an attempt to break it. "So I was thinking about hitting Macy's at lunchtime today," she said. She was wearing a short red skirt, with a V-neck rayon top. "Biannual storewide sale, you know? Anybody want to join me?" When no one answered, Paige continued. "What, did I miss somebody's funeral? What's up with you two this morning?"

"Just tired," Piper said, trying not to snap at her. She removed her coffee cup from the microwave and shot a glare Phoebe's way. "Not enough sleep."

"You could try drinking some of that coffee instead of just walking around with it," Paige told her.

"Some mornings there's just not enough coffee in the world," Phoebe mumbled. She looked as tired as Piper felt and had just slipped into some worn sweats for breakfast.

"Jeez, you guys," Paige said, sounding worried. "Cranky."

"Sorry," Piper replied. She carried her reheated coffee to the table and sat down with her back to her sisters.

Paige wasn't willing to let it drop, though. "I don't know what's up with you guys," she said. "Is it something I did?"

"No one's mad," Phoebe told her.

"Yeah. And none of us is female, either. Or brunettes."

"Paige?" Piper said without even turning to face her. "We're all really irritable this morning. Can we please just drop it? Okay?"

"Whatever," Paige said, her exasperation evident in her tone. She wrapped her bagel in a napkin and carried it to the door. "I'm late for work anyway. See ya." She stalked out, and slammed the front door behind her.

"You can't blame her for wondering," Phoebe said.

"You're the one who suspects her," Piper said.

"I don't suspect anything. I'm just concerned because of the vision. If you'd had it, you'd be concerned too."

"Now it's a vision?" Piper asked. "I thought last night it was a dream."

"Dream, vision, whatever. It came while I was asleep, and it had the internal consistency of a dream, which means not much. But it had the impact and clarity of a vision. And it really did lead us to that letter, you can't deny that. That's the main reason I give it any credence at all. The letter really was there."

Piper sipped her coffee, ignoring Phoebe. She knew that to some extent the continuation of the argument was her fault. She had taken the firm, unwavering position that Paige could be trusted, no matter what. Now each time Phoebe tried to push her to accept that the letter might possibly have some shred of validity, Piper dug in her heels even deeper. Every time she did that, Phoebe had to shove a little harder. She suspected Phoebe knew it too, but at this point they both were so committed to their stands that they couldn't even discuss a way around the stalemate. Something felt strange to her, *wrong*, about the way they both had chosen their ground over this and were sticking to it so firmly. But she couldn't quite put her finger on it and finally decided it was just because Phoebe was so clearly mistaken.

"I'm going upstairs," Phoebe announced after a moment, "to see what the *Book of Shadows* can tell us about dear old Great-Great-Great-Aunt Agnes."

"You do that," Piper said. She listened to Phoebe's footsteps on the stairs and felt a vast relief at being alone.

That relief lasted for all of three minutes, during which time she was able to figure out that she was just going to continue dwelling on the argument unless she did something to take her mind off it. She went into the next room and turned on a morning local news show. There was no shortage of bad news in her own daily life, what with innocents in trouble and demons on the prowl and the never-ending fight against evil, so it seemed pointless, and maybe even a bit redundant, to watch more bad news on TV. She flopped down on a floral sofa, put her coffee cup on the table—conveniently called a coffee table, she thought—and punched the power button on the remote.

When the screen flickered to life, there was a commercial on the screen for a long-distance phone service, featuring a man who stretched the very definition of the word comedian to the breaking point. Piper caught herself wondering if eliminating him would further the cause of good versus evil. *After all,* she thought, *he's assaulting the intelligence and good taste of every innocent who has the misfortune of being tuned in to this station.*

With a shimmering of light, Leo appeared beside her on the couch. "I love this guy," he said with a chuckle. Piper fixed him with a steely glare but decided not to press the issue. Mercifully the commercial ended.

"Where did you come from?" she asked him.

Leo ticked his eyes toward the ceiling.

"Pressing Whitelighter business?" she inquired. "I guess it's twenty-four/seven up there, huh?"

"No, upstairs," he answered.

"What, stairs aren't good enough for you anymore?"

"There's so much tension in the house I didn't want to run into Phoebe or Cole," he said. "You guys have got to work this thing out. And soon. How did it get so bad so fast?"

Piper shrugged and heaved a great sigh. "I don't know," she replied. "Just one of those things, I guess. But we'll get past it. We rarely argue about any one thing for more than a few days. This'll blow over too."

"Sooner is better than later. You never know when you'll all need to work together."

She shot him another withering look. "I know." Something on the TV caught her attention, a good thing because she'd turned it on to forget about her sisters for a few minutes, and then Leo had just come along and reminded her all over again.

". . . stabbed to death in Nob Hill last evening," the well-coiffed anchorwoman was saying. The picture cut to a scene shot the night before, bright lights washing a taped-off section of sidewalk as police technicians scoured it for clues. "In what many are speculating might be the work of a serial killer, this alleged victim seems to have been killed in identical fashion to the two previous stabbing victims discovered over the past few days. Police still have no clues, and no leads, to who allegedly murdered Julia Tilton, Sharlene Wells, or Gretchen Winter, or why."

"'Allegedly murdered,'" Piper quoted. "Since they were stabbed to death, then I think it's safe to say that they were *definitely* murdered."

"In the Tenderloin late last night, another grisly discovery," the newswoman announced, in a somber tone. The picture onscreen changed again, to coveralled investigators, wearing dust masks and goggles, lifting browned bones from the earth. "After plumbing problems flooded a nineteenth-century apartment building, nearly three dozen human skeletons were found buried beneath a basement floor. Investigators are still piecing together bones and bone fragments, trying to ascertain the exact number of people involved, before making any attempt to identify them. The bones seem to be at least a hundred years old, experts say, and perhaps even older. We'll keep you updated as more information is released."

"Eew," Piper said. "Who would bury a bunch of people underneath their apartment building?"

"No one who was acting within the law," Leo replied. "Unless funeral customs were a lot different then from now. I'd say they're looking at a hundred-year-old mass murder scene."

Piper was quiet for a moment, her mood, not particularly bright to begin with, made even more subdued by the two stories topping the news. "I guess there were serial killers in those days too," she said. "Jack the Ripper, right?"

"There were a few," Leo said. "He was the most famous, but there are others, too. H. H. Holmes in Chicago. Even John Wesley Hardin, the old western gunman, would fit the definition we use now. But . . ." He let his sentence trail off.

Piper elbowed him in the ribs. "But?"

"I don't know," he said somberly. "Just a

sense I get from seeing it on the screen, but I have this feeling that there's something not human at work here."

"A job for the Charmed Ones?"

Leo nodded slowly. "It could be. I think we need to take a closer look, at any rate."

Great, Piper thought. *I guess my sisters and I will have to cooperate whether we want to or not.* She glanced at Leo. *And how does he know such creepy stuff?*

The *Book of Shadows* was an amazing and often frustrating volume. Just about everything the Halliwell sisters would ever need to know to pursue their constant struggle against darkness was contained within its pages. But it was never the same book twice, and finding anything in it could prove a challenge. Sometimes the book would open itself to the needed page, but other times it was more obscure, and looking for a specific reference was like trying to find a pronounceable name in *War and Peace.*

When she first found the massive leather volume here in the attic and read the incantation that revived the Power of Three in her and her sisters, Phoebe had been royally freaked out. The unexpected appearance of the ghost of an ancestor, Melinda Warren, burned at the stake hundreds of years ago, had only added to her dismay. But since then, as they all had become more secure in their powers, and especially in those dark days after Prue's death, Phoebe had taken comfort in the attic and the presence of the book. Sometimes it seemed that as the youngest sister (though that role had since fallen to Paige, youngest chronologically as well as in experience with witchcraft), she had especially needed the feeling of connection she got here, the sense of continuity with all the Halliwell women who had come before. The understated light that streamed in through the stained-glass windows; the comforting familiarity of the brown leather book with the gold triquetra embossed on the front, three interlocking arcs contained in a ring; even the musty smells of old belongings, of history all put her at ease now.

Flipping through The *Book of Shadows*, though, Phoebe couldn't find any specific reference to however-many-greats Aunt Agnes. The book primarily contained spells and instructions on various witchy matters, but the sisters had, from time to time, found bits of family history in it when they needed to know something. Now, though, Phoebe became increasingly frustrated as she turned page after page and found nothing but the most glancing mentions. It was almost as if Agnes had been scrubbed from the book.

Finally, Phoebe had to recite a spell to get any concrete information to appear:

Pages left
And pages right
Bring Aunt Agnes's past
Into the light.

The *Book of Shadows* glowed for a moment with a light of its own, its leaves fluttered, and then the volume fell open to a page that Phoebe was certain hadn't been there before. It was a journal entry by yet another relative she had never heard of, Philippa Halliwell. The handwriting was old-fashioned and hard to read, but the Agnes letter had been too. Phoebe worked her way through it. Near the bottom of the page she found the reference she'd been looking for.

"Agnes came to the house for the first time since the day she turned against us," the spidery scrawl read. "We were polite, as she remains family, but no more than polite. She has brought disgrace upon the Halliwell family, and there are many among us who are not disposed to forgive her, nor will become so. Agnes, as the saying goes, has made her own bed. Whether she enjoys lying in it is not a concern for the rest of us."

Phoebe closed the book. *That's it?* she wondered. *The only reference to Great-Great-Great-Aunt Agnes the* Book of Shadows *can come up with? Talk about useless.*

So old Agnes was on the outs with the rest of the family. That was good to know, she supposed, but it didn't really explain anything about the warning she had hidden in the back of that old bureau. In a way, maybe it even supported Piper's viewpoint. If Agnes had been a troublemaker of some kind, perhaps the warning was phony. Or maybe it had to do with whatever the woman had done that made the rest of the family turn against her, in which case it was nothing but ancient history now. The idea occurred to her to summon Agnes herself, but she quickly decided against it. If the rift between Agnes and the other Halliwells had been serious enough, she might be inviting disaster into their midst.

Phoebe sat down on the attic floor, feeling alone and lost. There had been a time when Piper had been the peacemaker, running interference whenever she had an argument with Prue, which had been, she had to admit, frequently. But Piper was the problem now, and with Paige the subject of the disagreement, there were no remaining sisters she could talk to. Cole had taken her side, but then he would. She needed someone less biased to use as a sounding board, and there wasn't anyone available. She was on her own with this one.

At the Social Services office, Bob Cowan, Paige's boss, was in one of his moods. There were days, and this looked to be one of them, when she thought he could use a social worker himself, preferably one who would steer him into an anger management program. *Maybe it takes a hair-trigger temper and the ability to nurse a grudge to be a boss,* she thought. *You just need that right ratio of obnoxious, condescending, and overbearing to be able to treat people like they are your personal property, beholden to you for all the blessings you bestowed upon them and for looking to you for direction and guidance.*

Or at least, maybe that was what Mr. Cowan believed. He certainly seemed to regard his position as some sort of feudal lordship, and himself as the lord, responsible for his own personal fiefdom. She had no doubt that if he could get away with it, he'd institute the stocks, and maybe death by guillotine as legitimate forms of punishment for such transgressions as failing to fill out paperwork properly, forgetting to refill the stapler when it ran out, and, worst of all, demonstrating unacceptable amounts of attitude in his lordship's presence.

Paige figured she was making a bit too much of his snapping in her general direction, almost forty minutes ago. To be fair, she had forgotten to write an appointment in his calendar, resulting in two families, equally needy, showing up at the office at the same time expecting to be able to sit down with Mr. Cowan.

The good thing about Mr. Cowan—the thing that kept Paige here working for him, instead of turning her back on the place and finding a new career, maybe even one that paid a living San Francisco wage—was that he had not only the smarts and resources to help people but the drive to do it no matter what. He was a tyrant sometimes, but in the service of something Paige truly believed was worth doing. Sometimes people just needed a helping hand, a push in the right direction, a little guidance. It wasn't their fault that luck had run against them, that they found themselves on the wrong side of the ever-growing divide between the haves and have-nots. Bob Cowan understood that, and he put his beliefs to the test on the front lines of the struggle everyday. As annoyed as Paige got with him, she could never allow herself to forget that.

Anyway, she knew that today she was really ticked at her own sisters and just projecting that annoyance at everyone else. Especially Cowan. She didn't know what had been going on in the house this morning, but it was clear that it had something to do with her. The way Phoebe and Piper had both been so artificially pleasant to her, all the while shooting eye daggers at each other when they thought she wasn't looking . . . something was definitely bothering the Halliwell sisters. And maybe their respective guys, too; Leo and Cole both had kept themselves very scarce all morning. *Why couldn't they just come out and talk to me about it?* she wondered. *It's not like I'm hard to approach or anything. Is it?*

No, they were more than happy to talk to her—at length even—when she was doing something that bugged them. So this time it wasn't anything as simple as some bad habit of hers grating on them. Something deeper was going on. Something more troubling.

Which just makes it that much more important for them to come right out and address it, she thought, *instead of tiptoeing around it and putting everyone in a foul mood.*

The more she dwelled on it, the worse her own mood became. She found herself looking forward to her lunch break, not just because she planned to spend time looking at outfits she couldn't hope to afford but because she'd be away from the office for a while, someplace where if she bit anybody's head off, at least it would more likely be a stranger's than a co-worker's.

At this point she'd be happy with that small blessing.

Chapter

3

"I have to tell her, Cole," Phoebe insisted. They were in her room, where she'd found her ex-demon boyfriend waiting for her. Cole was tall, dark, and oh-so-handsome, and while she had a problem with the fact that there had been a time when he could turn into Belthazor at the drop of a hat and had wanted to kill the Halliwell sisters, she had to admit that his bad-boy edge had a definite appeal. As long as he wasn't *too* bad.

"Tell her what?" he demanded, pacing in front of the bed Phoebe sat on. "I thought you didn't learn anything."

"Almost nothing," Phoebe told him. "But that in itself tells us something, right? If old Agnes was so disliked by the family that there's hardly even any record of her in the *Book of Shadows*, that is meaningful information."

"Meaningful noninformation, maybe," Cole

muttered. "Not necessarily what I'd call helpful. But if you want to tell Piper, go ahead. She's your sister. Just don't be surprised when she isn't persuaded."

"Piper's not like that, Cole," she replied. "At least, not usually. Although today I guess anything could happen."

Cole simply shrugged.

"Ha!" Piper laughed. "There you go."

Phoebe and Cole had found Piper and Leo downstairs in the kitchen, talking about something that seemed important but that they hadn't bothered to share. Phoebe had told them what little she'd learned from the *Book of Shadows*: that Great-Great-Great-Aunt Agnes had done something that had turned the rest of the Halliwells against her and that if the family had ever found it in its heart to forgive her, that information had been somehow left out of the book. She had even revealed how hard it was to find anything at all about Agnes in the book and that she'd had to use magic to make even that tiny bit of info show up.

Cole had, she hated to admit, pegged Piper's response just right.

"So I guess that shoots your theory down in flames, doesn't it?" Piper asked. "I mean, if we were meant to take the warning seriously, don't you think it would have come from someone a little more trustworthy?"

"We don't know that she's not trustworthy," Phoebe replied, realizing the hopelessness of her statement even as she uttered it.

"No, because probably all the rest of the Halliwells were evil then, and Agnes was the only good one. Look, Phoebe, if the family turned against her, she must have done something bad. Really bad. And if she's really bad, I don't see how we can take her word for it that Paige is up to no good, even if we *could* agree that her warning applies to Paige, which we can't."

"I understand your point of view, Piper, really." Phoebe turned one of the kitchen chairs around and sat down on it backward, straddling the seat. "You know I've accepted Paige into this family from the beginning."

"Against my advice," Cole said.

"Well, you weren't necessarily the most reliable source, for a while there," Leo observed. To say that Cole and Paige had not warmed to each other immediately was an understatement.

"We all have accepted Paige," Piper declared. "So I don't think it's a good idea to go around *un*accepting her now."

"That's not fair!" Phoebe cried. "You know that's not what I'm saying. I'm just saying that something told me to look in that chest. I did, and we found the letter there. These things don't just happen, Piper, unless there's a reason for it. You know that's not how it works. We just ought to investigate a little more, that's all."

"Great Aunt Agnes has been dead for . . . I don't know . . . decades anyway, right? We've never even heard of her before, and it sounds like for good reason. Why should we doubt our own sister just because of something she might have written and hidden away who knows how long ago? It's ancient history, Phoebe. Let it go."

Phoebe felt Piper's words like a knife in the heart. It was hard enough for her even to suggest that Paige might not be entirely trustworthy. She felt incredibly guilty about bringing it up again. But the more Piper pooh-poohed the idea, the more strongly she found herself thinking that it had merit. Paige *had* pretty much come out of nowhere, and they had taken her in because she was a half sister. But maybe there was some benefit to be derived from making the sisters feel secure in the Power of Three, only to turn on them at some later date.

"Piper's right, Phoebe," Leo added with firm certainty. "I'd know if Paige was anything but what she says she is. She's your mother's daughter, with a Whitelighter father. I can see that in her."

"Which doesn't mean she's trustworthy. There was a time when you couldn't see the demon in me," Cole told him.

"Maybe I just didn't want to," Leo snapped back. "Maybe I wanted to trust the impressions of Piper and her sisters."

"But you won't do that now?" Cole demanded.

Leo rose from his seat at the kitchen table, a rare scowl darkening his features. Phoebe knew Cole, with a history of evil, was more the scowling type, while Leo was generally Mr. Sunshine. "I'm still trusting in Piper and one sister. I'm just having a little trouble with the other."

"Could be you're basing your trust on who you like most, rather than on the evidence," Cole said. He paced the kitchen floor as he might have done a courtroom in his attorney days. "As an ADA I had to fight against that all the time. Defendants do their best to be more likable than lawyers, so the jury will side with them over those of us trying to prosecute them. But this could be important, Leo, really important. You need to put aside your bias and look at the facts."

"The fact is, you and Phoebe have nothing."

"That's not so!" Phoebe burst out, slamming the tabletop with her palm. She had to blink back tears of frustration and rage. "I had a *premonition*, okay? It led me to that dresser that we've all seen a million times but never paid the slightest bit of attention to. And it was such a powerful vision I couldn't just ignore it. I woke up Cole, and we went up and tore the dresser apart on the spot."

"I know," Piper said. "I remember the part about losing sleep from all the noise you guys made. But it was not a premonition, as you said at the time. It was a *dream*."

"Whatever. I like my sleep too," Phoebe told her. "You think I'd get out of bed for something like that if I didn't have the sense that it was vital?"

"Probably not," Piper answered.

"Definitely not. And the letter was there, and it was real. It's in my room. You can still read it if you want. Aunt Agnes was real—not popular, maybe, but real. So the possibility that Paige may not be as trustworthy as we think she is—that's real too."

"Well stated," Cole told her. He looked at Leo and Piper, who were both watching and looking a little shellshocked. "And the jury's verdict?"

Piper started to answer, but Leo gripped her shoulder, silencing her, and spoke instead. "The jury is taking a recess. You guys came in just as we were getting ready to leave. We've given you as much time as we can, but we really have someplace we have to be. We'll take this up again some other time."

Before Cole or Phoebe could object, there was a spray of glittering lights, like sparks flashing and dying around a campfire, and Leo and Piper had vanished, orbed away by Leo's Whitelighter power.

"Well, that was rude," Phoebe said simply.

Cole just harrumphed and sat back down at the table, rubbing his right fist with his left hand as if he wanted to hit somebody.

Probably, Phoebe thought, *he does.*

• • •

Piper and Leo appeared just outside the hundred-year-old crime scene that had made the news that morning. The old building was surrounded by yellow police tape, wrapped around stanchions, keeping the curious at bay. Several police cars and vans were parked at odd angles around the area. Uniformed cops looked bored, talking to one another or standing with arms crossed, gazing off at nothing in particular. Piper quickly scanned faces, knowing that if anyone had spotted them orbing in, it would show. No one had, and that was good. Leo could make people forget, if he had to, but the power was hard to control, and they might find that they had forgotten other, more pertinent facts, such as spouses' birthdays or their own names.

She hadn't liked leaving without telling Phoebe where they were going, or why. But so far they didn't know there was anything supernatural going on here. All they had was Leo's hunch, and he wasn't very sure about it. Considering the way she and Phoebe had been feeling about each other, and the way she'd been dismissive of Phoebe's hunch, she didn't want to say anything about this to her sisters until she knew what was up.

The three-story building was a massive turn-of-the-twentieth-century red sandstone structure. A couple of stores occupied street-level spaces, with what looked like apartments above.

Next door, on the uphill side, was a clapboard house obviously undergoing significant renovation. Scaffolding stood against its exterior wall, and paint had been stripped from its surface. Windows and trim were taped for painting.

From a wide double door of the sandstone, Piper noticed with a grimace, a procession of men and women carried zipped-up rubber body bags to waiting vans.

"It's called the Gates Mansion," a voice from behind them said. They turned to see Darryl Morris, a detective with the SFPD and one of the few mortals who knew the Halliwell sisters were witches. Piper had always thought he was a handsome man, and the pale blue shirt he wore under a navy suit made for a nice contrast with his rich dark skin. It had been the wrong thing to wear today, though. The pants were stained and filthy below the knees. He'd have been better off in jeans or coveralls like those the workers with the body bags wore. "After Herman Gates, a nineteenth-century entrepreneur. No relation to Bill. He built the place in 1884 as a combined doctor's office and pharmacy, with apartments above. He lived in one wing and leased out all the rest, which is the kind of thinking that made him rich but keeps the rest of us poor. It's one of the oldest examples of its kind in the city and one of the best ones to survive the 1906 earthquake."

Every San Franciscan knew about the quake,

as did most other Americans. It leveled large swaths of the city, and resulting fires, burning out of control since the city's water supply had been largely cut off by the quake, took out most of the rest. Though the city had been around since the mid-1800s, most of its current buildings had gone up sometime after 1906.

"It's kind of spooky-looking," Piper commented.

"Said the lady who lives in a house of witches," Darryl replied.

"But not scary witches. Good witches."

"The best," Leo added.

She leaned into him, enjoying the comfortable feel and smell of him as she did. "Thanks."

"So do you have a professional interest in this?" Darryl asked. "Or just morbid curiosity?"

"We get enough 'morbid' in our daily life not to be overly curious," Piper said.

"Just a hunch," Leo added. "Something felt odd to me when I saw the report on TV."

"Want to take a look around?" Darryl asked.

That, of course, was exactly the offer Piper had been waiting for. "Can we, Darryl?"

"I think there are so many people working this scene that no one would notice a couple more, especially if they're with me. Come on." Darryl raised the crime scene tape, and they all passed underneath.

When Leo spoke again, as they waited for a couple of techs to come out the door with yet

another body bag in their hands, his voice was
low and solemn. "What happened here,
Darryl?"

Darryl tipped his head toward the building
next door. "Renovations on that clapboard," he
said. "Thing's been painted so many times it
looks like a bag of jelly beans where they're
scraping through the layers. Last week the
plumbers were in, and the pipes they were
working on—probably original to the building—burst. Water came flowing out, ran down-
hill, and got into the Gates place. Which, as I
said, is a historical landmark."

When the doorway was clear, Darryl led
them inside. The big doors opened onto an
entryway that was surprisingly small, considering the size of the edifice. But Darryl had said
the building had several uses, so Mr. Gates probably wouldn't have wanted to devote a lot of
space to a grand entryway. Piper could see that
the marble floor was streaked and dirty.

"When Gates died, in 1897, the wing that he
had occupied was turned into apartments,
including the basement, which he had insisted
on since he came from the Midwest, where tor-
nadoes were much more serious concerns than
earthquakes. He had no heirs and no will, and
the city eventually took possession of the property. It didn't really have any need for a big
house down here, but even then low-income
housing was always at a premium."

"So the water," Leo said as they walked farther into the dark, musty place, "seeking the lowest point . . ."

"Flowed into the basement." Darryl finished Leo's speculation. "Which has no drainage."

"That'd be a mess," Piper said.

"That's not the worst of it," Darryl told her. He took them to a low doorway, barely six feet tall, Piper guessed, that opened onto a narrow flight of stairs. "The floor down there was a plain concrete slab, not very well laid. There were cracks. Water went into the cracks. The caretaker thought he was going to have a big cleanup job, vacuuming the water out, but when he got the equipment down there, the water was gone. Which meant it had soaked down underneath the floor."

They started down the narrow stairs. A wooden banister was bolted to the block wall on one side, and a couple of light bulbs, connected by exposed wire, illuminated the staircase. From below a rank, sickly sweet smell rose up to meet them. *Geesh*, Piper thought, *that's nasty.*

"And the caretaker was worried about what might be under the concrete?" Leo asked. Always the handyman.

"The caretaker put his fingers into one of the cracks and pulled, and the concrete came right up," Darryl informed them. "Stuff was just poured on top of a dirt floor, and not a very even one at that. When the water soaked the dirt and concrete, it loosened up, and the guy was able to lift whole chunks of it. That's when he saw the bones."

"We knew there were bones somewhere in the story," Piper said. "We saw that much on TV."

Darryl reached the concrete floor, still intact for a couple of feet at the bottom of the steps, and pointed to something that Piper couldn't quite see yet. She came down the rest of the way and, leaning forward, peered over the lip of solid concrete floor into the trench that had been dug there.

And was immediately sorry she had.

As Darryl had described, the concrete floor had come up in relatively small pieces, which were piled around the perimeter of the wall. The rest was dirt, which may have been disturbed by the water but had been further disturbed by workers with shovels, trowels, and brushes, all still in evidence. The workers, men and women both, wore hazmat suits that covered their faces and kept them safe from any airborne nasties that might be floating around down there. *Which is more than I can say for us*, Piper thought. *We're just down here in our street clothes, and who knows* what *we're breathing in?* Working mostly on hands and knees, the crew carefully scraped dirt, millimeters at a time, until they found bones. Piper could see bone jutting up through the earth nearly everywhere she looked. It wasn't clean and white, like the models in doctors' offices, but had taken on the brown of the surrounding dirt, making it look incredibly ancient to her.

And human. Definitely human.

"Darryl," she said, "how many . . ."

"We're at forty-six confirmed, and still counting," Darryl said, "where we've got either skulls or enough skeletal parts to guarantee each unique victim."

"Victim?" Leo asked. "Isn't that still speculation?"

"This is not a registered cemetery," Darryl replied. "No one lawfully buried fifty people down here. This is a murder scene, or at least the aftermath, a place where murders were concealed by burial. Those are victims."

"Do you know how old they are?" Piper asked.

"We're still running some tests," Darryl said. "But we're guessing twentieth century. I guess that doesn't say much, does it? Turn of the century, early on, maybe '04, '05. Somewhere around there."

Piper noticed that Leo had almost fallen into a trance. He stared at the brown earth and the bones and the people working at digging them up, but his eyes were unfocused, as if he were seeing right through them to something else, something Piper couldn't hope to grasp. "Leo?" she asked.

He blinked and nodded his head, as if he'd just woken up. "Sorry."

"What is it?"

"That sense I had, that there was something . . . not quite natural about all this?"

"What about it?"

"It's back," Leo said. "In a big way."

Darryl turned to face them and kept his voice low, so as not to be overheard. "If you think there's something supernatural going on here, go ahead and try to figure it out," he said. "But not here. You guys can't stay down here without me, and I've got to leave. If you come up with anything, let me know before you make a move. And I do mean before."

"Got it, Darryl," Piper told him. "No worries."

"There are always worries where the Charmed Ones are concerned," Darryl fired back. "But I've got other worries of my own right now."

"Worse than this?" she asked him.

"More pressing," he said. "These killings happened a hundred years ago, give or take. But last night I caught a case of a killing that happened, well, last night. The third in a series."

Piper figured he must have meant the one they had seen on TV that morning, the three women who had been "allegedly murdered." But Leo didn't let on that they knew anything about it. "What was that one like?" Leo asked.

"Seemingly random, crime of opportunity, no apparent motive. Young woman stabbed to death on her way to work at a restaurant. No robbery, no witnesses. She didn't have an angry ex-boyfriend or a jealous current one. Didn't seem to have any enemies at all that we could tell. But someone took her out, savagely, on the street. Multiple stab wounds, by a knife we haven't found and can't quite identify. No marks, no fingerprints, nothing else notable about the scene, except that she was wet."

"Wet?" Piper asked. "It was foggy last night, right?"

"More than that, though. As if she'd been splashed or soaked by something. Patches of moisture on her collar, on her shoulder, on her sleeve."

"Makes no sense," Leo said.

"Exactly," Darryl replied. "And that's why I have to leave now. This is a horrible crime, but it's over. We're thinking whoever did the one last night, and a couple before that, is just getting started."

The manor was empty when they got back, a relief to Piper. The last thing she wanted, after such a grim morning, was another stupid run-in with Phoebe over the stupid Aunt Agnes letter. She and Leo parked themselves on the couch, where they had caught the story of the bodies on TV just that morning. It seemed ages ago already.

"Are you thinking what I'm thinking?" Leo asked her.

"Almost never, it seems," Piper said. "Except when we're both in a romantic mood. Which, if you are now, yuck. No, thanks."

"Not at all," Leo said, greatly relieving her. "I'm wondering if there's more than just coincidence at work here."

Piper didn't follow his reasoning. "At work where?"

"The bodies at the Gates Mansion," he answered, "and the case that Darryl is investigating, the murder last night, and the two before that."

She shook her head. "Not that a murder is ever a good thing. But some of them are less, you know, supernaturally oriented than others. Those just sound like murders to me."

"But they don't to me," Leo said. "What did he say? No motive, no witnesses, they aren't even quite sure what the murder weapon is, just something that somebody used to stab her. Multiple times, he said."

"So what makes them supernatural?"

"Police these days are pretty good at collecting physical evidence," Leo said. He was gazing off into space again, as if trying to visualize the scene as he talked about it. "Very good, in fact. There should be something. If she tried to defend herself, maybe some of the killer's skin under her nails. If he held her while he stabbed her, which he'd almost have to do to pull the weapon out and stab again and again, there should be prints, hair, sweat—some kind of DNA evidence. Since there were no witnesses, it all must have happened pretty fast. He would have taken off, not hung around long enough to go over her corpse with a fine-tooth comb, removing every last flake of skin that could tie them together. And if it's odd that it happened once, it's especially curious if it happened three times in a row."

"I think you're reaching here, Leo," Piper told him. For some reason it seemed as if everyone around her were trying to involve her in things that weren't necessarily her concern: Phoebe's Aunt Agnes letter and now Leo's hunch. "After all, Darryl said the murders at the Gates place were committed a hundred years ago. How does that tie in with killings that happened this week?"

He nodded, still looking kind of distracted. "I know. I'm not saying they're definitely connected. I'm just saying, what if they are? I feel like there's a supernatural component to the Gates Mansion killings, and there could well be one to the other murders."

She wasn't willing to give in yet, but she decided at least to entertain the possibility that he was right. "If they are linked, then I'd say it's something the Power of Three should be looking into."

"Sounds like it."

"Maybe we can find the killer," Piper said. "Scrying, anyone?"

They went up to the attic, and Piper spread out the map of San Francisco they kept for just such occasions. Holding a crystal pendulum above the map's center, she concentrated, trying to empty her mind except for a vision of the murder scene as Darryl had described it, with some extra geographical details they'd picked up from that day's paper. The story had been brief, just a police blotter item, but there had been an address and a small picture of the most recent victim, Julia Tilton. *I hope,* Piper thought, *that's all I'll need to get a bead on the guy.* She knew there was no guarantee, not without some physical aspect of the killer to home in on. But as Leo had said, the police hadn't found the slightest trace of physical evidence, so this was as good as she was going to get for now.

She focused, willing her mental energy through the crystal. She could almost see the scene in her mind's eye, the steep hillside street, the dark buildings, the frantic late-for-work dash, the fog . . .

The string went taut and the crystal started to move. "Got something," she said under her breath. Beside her she felt the presence of Leo, watching closely.

The crystal hovered over the Embarcadero, stretching the string she held to its limit. "Looks like Battery and Lombard," she said excitedly.

But even as she spoke, the crystal swung wildly, coming to a stop over Golden Gate Park. "No, wait. The park."

And it swung again, to Nob Hill, stopped there momentarily and then once more, to the Western Addition, then came all the way back around to Russian Hill.

"This doesn't make sense," Piper said. "It's like it has locked in on something, but something that's everywhere at once."

"Or incredibly fast," Leo said.

"That's it," Piper said, a sarcastic edge in her voice. "We're looking for Speedy Gonzales. It's not supernatural; it's just a cartoon mouse." She put the useless crystal down. "It isn't working. If it's really found someone, he's all over the city." She stood up, feeling dejected, and Leo embraced her. That helped.

And outside, fog settled once again over the city. . . .

Chapter

4

Union Square was its usual chaotic self. Even on this cool, foggy day, the square was jammed. Tourists stared up at the memorial tower, the purpose of which Paige could never quite remember but that she thought had something to do with Admiral Dewey, whoever he was; street musicians jammed on the sidewalks and benches; a mime infuriated passersby with his impressions of them. The street in front of the St. Francis Hotel was packed with taxis and limousines, and the many flags over its entryway drooped damply over their poles instead of flapping in the wind. The sidewalks all around the square were thick with pedestrians, many carrying shopping bags from the big department stores, Macy's or Neiman Marcus, or the boutiques, like Gucci and Armani, that lined the streets. The air was thick with the smells that characterized the city for Paige: exhaust and tobacco, exotic foods and coffees from all the restaurants, a variety of perfumes and colognes. This was truly an international city, and Paige saw and heard people of every race and description on the streets.

She tugged her sweater tighter around herself to ward off the chill and wished momentarily that she had worn a longer skirt or even pants. But then she glanced into a shopwindow and caught a glimpse of a handsome young man gazing admiringly at her legs, and she remembered why she wore short skirts to begin with. *If you've got it, go with it*, she believed.

Macy's had been a bust, unfortunately. Because of the sale, it had been even more crowded than usual, something that she would barely have believed possible—except during the holiday season, when it seemed to contain more warm bodies than many small countries. It wasn't where she usually shopped, but there were some special pieces she liked there, including a really great pair of spiky boots she just loved. But even when she had been able to get close to the things she wanted to see, the prices had still remained out of reach for her. Somehow, even after moving into the manor Grams had left them, with Piper and Phoebe, Paige didn't seem to be able to put any money aside at the end of the month. She had finally given up on shopping and gone down to the food court on the lower level, had a salad, and was on her way back to work, waiting for a cable car to come up Powell.

The corner of Powell and O'Farrell was of course utterly packed. People bustled by in every direction, bumping into her, excusing themselves, swerving at the last second. Paige waited, dodging and smiling at the people, as she tried to stay out of their way. Getting a cable car, she knew, would be an iffy proposition; half the time there was a line down at the terminus, and by the time the cars made it to the first stop, they were already at capacity. She could walk a couple of blocks over and catch a bus, but she wanted to try for the car first. It was more fun and ultimately quicker if she could get on right away.

Sidestepping around a blind woman with a white cane and really lovely silver hair, Paige noticed another woman, standing by the corner chatting into a cell phone. A little boy held on to the woman's free hand, and with his other hand he bounced a red rubber ball on the sidewalk. Bounce and catch, bounce and catch. He couldn't have been more than three, Paige guessed, a cute towhead with a mischievous smile and gigantic blue eyes. *Grow up to be one of the good ones*, Paige wished in his direction.

As she watched, he bounced the ball and grabbed for it but missed. It took another bounce, away from him, and then ricocheted off

someone's knee and caromed off a wall. The boy
tugged free of his mother's hand and started
after it.

The mother didn't even seem to notice that
her boy was gone. She continued her chat, obliv-
ious of his absence, even though she was now
able to switch hands and ears. Paige spun
around to watch the boy, who took a few hesitant steps after his ball. He was plenty old
enough to walk, she noted, but probably not to
watch for traffic on busy downtown streets. And
his legs weren't long enough to enable him to
catch the ball in time. If it kept bouncing, it could
easily go all the way down Powell to Ellis. If the
kid followed it into the cross street, he'd never
make it to his fourth birthday.

She took a quick glance around to make sure
no one was paying attention to her. So far the
boy's predicament seemed to have gone unnoticed by the throng. Everyone was too wrapped
up in his or her own life to notice something
occurring at knee level, and the fog was too thick
for anyone to see from a distance. Satisfied that
she was unobserved, Paige orbed the ball backward, and floated it gently into the boy's hands.
He watched, delighted, as his ball drifted right
to him, and when he caught it, he gripped it
tightly in both hands, a huge smile spreading
across his face. With the innocence of youth, he
didn't even seem to question how it had happened, just laughed once and ran back up the

hill to his mother. As he got there, the light at
O'Farrell changed and the woman took his hand
again and crossed toward the square. She would
never know he'd been gone.

I'm not too happy about that part, Paige thought.
*I wish there were a way I could let her know what she
had almost done, by being careless.* But she couldn't
think of anything that wouldn't give away her
own secret or that would be believed, and the
important thing was that the boy was safe now.
Maybe he'd learned something, even if his
mother had not.

Paige had turned away to look into a shopwindow when she caught the reflection of a young
man stepping from the fog and approaching her, a
friendly smile on his face. *And what a face*, Paige
thought as she spun around for a clearer view. His
twinkling eyes were gray, almost the exact color of
the fog. His chin was firm, jawline strong, mouth
fixed in a kind of cockeyed half grin that was at
once endearing and disarming. He was tall, with
spiked blond hair and a muscular build, accentu-
ated by a short-sleeved silk shirt and dress pants,
both in shades of gray.

And he's coming right toward me, she thought.
She was still trying to convince herself that she
was wrong when he stopped in front of her and
spoke.

"That was great, what you did," he said.

She decided to play dumb. "What I did?
What do you mean?"

"You know," he said, gesturing as if he were orbing a bouncing ball. "The kid, the ball. That whole hero thing. I'm impressed."

"I'm sorry." Paige lied. "I don't know what you're talking about."

"It's okay," he told her. His smile didn't budge as he talked to her, didn't waver. "I'm one too."

"One what?"

He leaned in close, whispering so only she could hear. "A witch."

"You are?" she asked, startled. Then, catching herself, she added, "I didn't think there were real witches."

"Of course there are," he said. "I'm Timothy." She thought he'd put out his hand to shake, but he didn't, just crammed both his hands into the rear pockets of his pants. He bobbed his upper body toward her in an awkward half bow. "I'm Timothy, and I'm a witch."

"I'm Paige," she said. "Paige Matthews."

"And you're a witch."

"You make it sound like some kind of twelve-step program." She laughed nervously. "Anyway, I'm not a witch."

"Paige, I saw what you did." He pantomimed it again. "It was brilliant."

"But . . ."

"You can admit it to me," he said. "It's not like witchcraft is any big secret to other witches, right?"

The cable car came then, and Paige thought that maybe she'd be delivered from this very awkward conversation with this very attractive man. But the car was full and didn't even slow down at her stop.

"Look, there's a café right here," Timothy said. "Let's grab one of these outside tables and have a cup, and we can talk about it."

"About what?" she asked, playing dumb again.

He just scooted a chair back for her and gestured her into it. "I really have to get back to work," she protested meekly.

"It'll just be a few minutes," Timothy insisted. "You missed the cable car anyway."

"But I can catch a bus."

"There'll be another bus in ten minutes. You won't be that late."

She could scarcely believe she was fighting so hard to get away from this guy. He was gorgeous, and normally she'd have worked this hard just to get close to him. But the fact that he knew she was a witch freaked her out far more than she would have believed. *Weren't you just wishing there were a guy who would understand?* she asked herself. *Isn't it possible that this is that guy?*

But instead of being drawn to him, she just wanted to run away.

She didn't, though. He disappeared into the coffee shop for a minute, and she sat there waiting, watching the parade of bodies pass by on the mobbed sidewalk, cutting through fog that clung to them like strands of thick webbing. Even the fact that there was a free table at this café seemed like more than just happenstance, like part of some vast conspiracy, a web designed to trap her. And it wasn't that she objected to being trapped . . .

A moment later he reappeared next to the table. She hadn't even heard him approach, and his hands were empty. The look on his face was one of deep embarrassment. "I, uh, I forgot, when I asked you to coffee," he said, mumbling toward the sidewalk. "I actually walked away from home without my wallet this morning." He patted the pockets of his pants, as if offering proof. "I'm financially humiliated."

"That's okay," Paige told him. "I can buy, this time." She sat up, and he took the chair opposite hers.

"I'll hold our table," he said.

She cast a final look back at him as she passed through the swinging door. Inside, soft jazz played on a hidden stereo system, and the odors of coffee and cinnamon and steamed milk tickled her senses. The place was crowded, with families sitting around tables deep in conversation, solo caffeine addicts leafing through the *Chronicle*, young couples lost in each other's presence. Paige got in line and then realized she hadn't even asked Timothy what he wanted.

Well, she thought, *he didn't ask me either. So I guess he'll just take what I give him, and like it.*

A few minutes later she backed through the swinging doors, burning hot paper cups of cappuccino in each hand. She put them on the table and sat down.

"Perfect," Timothy said with a smile. "Thanks. I am deeply sorry."

"It's no problem, really," she told him. "It's just a cup of coffee."

"It's a cup of coffee and a principle," he said. "If I invite you to join me for something, I should be able to pay for it."

Paige took a sip of the hot drink, wanting to change the subject so he'd quit apologizing for nothing. "So, you're really a witch?" she asked.

He tossed her a grin and held up his hands, levitating his coffee cup off the table several inches, then lowering it back down gently. "I get by," he said. "When I saw the kid lose the ball, I was about to try something, but you really nailed it."

"What would you have done?"

"I was trying to come up with a spell to stop the bouncing ball. Then either the kid could have caught up to it, or I could have grabbed it and handed it to him."

"That would have worked."

"But not with the elegance of yours." He smiled again and tapped his cup against hers in a kind of toast. "That was some move. You must be very powerful."

Paige remembered what she'd been told about the Power of Three. The Charmed Ones were, according to the *Book of Shadows,* the most powerful witches of all time. As long as there were three of them, that was. If anything happened to one, then they'd lose the Power of Three and their abilities would be severely impacted. That was why they had to be on their guard at all times; there were plenty of warlocks and demons who would love to take even one of them out, weakening the whole. And that was why her discovering her sisters had been so important after Prue had died; it meant there still could be a Power of Three.

So even if he suspected—strongly—that she was a witch, she wasn't about to tell him that she was one of the Charmed Ones. At least until she knew him better. A *lot* better.

And the prospect of knowing him better, she thought, *is starting to be kind of appealing.*

She sipped her coffee, getting foam on her nose, and laughed when she wiped it off.

"That's good, I like that," Timothy said. He was watching her closely, as if she might vanish at any moment. That she could do, of course, but she wasn't about to let Timothy know that.

"What do you mean?"

"Laughing," he said. "I get the feeling you haven't had the greatest day so far."

"It's been okay," she told him.

"No, it hasn't."

"Hey, whose day is it?" she asked, laughing again.

"Yours," Timothy replied. "But empathy, I guess, is one of my gifts. I can kind of tell about things like that, and your day has been mostly sucky."

She tried to plumb the depths of his eyes, to see if she could tell anything like that about him. But empathy, she guessed, was not one of her own powers. "Okay," she said finally. "You're right. It hasn't been the greatest."

"What's wrong?" he asked. "Never mind, I'm prying. Bad habit. I get too involved, too easily. Especially when I like someone."

"You just met me. How can you like me?"

"I met you *because* I saw you save a little kid's life. And you're adorable. What's not to like?"

She looked down, into her coffee cup. She couldn't believe this guy was coming on so strong. More than that, she couldn't believe she was trying so hard to resist a guy who was coming on so strong, especially one who fitted all her major qualifications. *Male, handsome, knows about witch stuff and doesn't freak out, and did I mention male?*

She decided the best way to change the subject was to get back to his original question. "Family problems, I guess," she said, figuring that didn't give away too much.

"Parents?"

"Siblings. They're arguing, but they won't tell

me what about. Which makes me think it's about me."

"Because if it wasn't, they'd all be trying to get you on their side."

He really gets it, she thought. "Exactly."

"So you really have no idea what the nature of the argument is?"

"It could be a lot of things, I guess," she said. "Paige is an airhead. Paige isn't pulling her weight with the household chores. Paige doesn't respect boundaries. Paige talks before she thinks—guess I'm proving that one right now, huh?"

She noticed that Timothy wasn't smiling anymore, was in fact frowning, his mouth turned down and his smooth brow furrowed like a freshly plowed field. "You shouldn't be so hard on yourself," he said. "I get the feeling you're a much tougher critic of yourself than your siblings are."

She shrugged, took another sip of the coffee. "I really should go catch that bus," she said.

He looked stricken. "I don't mean to be so nosy. Just tell me when I've gone over the line, and I'll back off. I'm good at that. I've had lots of practice."

It was Paige's turn to smile. "Now who's being hard on himself?"

"See?" he said, flashing her a grin she felt down to her toes. "We all do it sometimes. We just have to be careful not to put too much stock in it."

"I'm not usually that way," she told him. "I mean, sometimes I am, when I get really down about something. But more often I'm, like, the bubbly one, you know? So cheerful that other people get sick of it. Especially if it's early in the morning."

"Well, you've got a lot to be happy about," Timothy said.

"You think so?" She didn't know how he could figure that out but thought it was worth seeing if he had any reason or was just feeding her a line. She was voting for line so far.

"Sure. You're beautiful and apparently healthy. You have clothes that look terrific on you. You have family who care about you enough to fight about you and try to spare you at the same time. You have a job you care enough about that you're concerned about getting back from lunch late. You're a powerful witch who uses her abilities for good. Sounds like a completely excellent life to me."

So, both. He was feeding her a line—but what a line! It all sounded so right when he said it, so true. She really didn't have much to complain about. So she couldn't afford new outfits at the department stores that often. There were more important things than cool new boots.

And that job he'd mentioned really was a good one, but she wouldn't have it for long if she didn't get back there. She stood up. "Timothy, I'm very glad I met you."

"I'm glad too, Paige," he said. "Glad I saw you help that kid. Do you really have to go so soon?"

"I really do," she replied.

"Can I . . . call you sometime?"

Sometime soon, she hoped. But she hesitated. He'd proved that he had some powers, but she still didn't want to confirm his suspicions about her. Even if he *had* observed her at work.

"If you're worried about my revealing your secret, you don't have to be," he said, almost as if he'd read her mind. "I'm very discreet."

Finally, Paige tugged a pen from her back-pack and wrote her work phone number down on a napkin, then folded it and slid it across the table toward him. When he didn't take it immediately, she removed her hand. Then he scooped it up and pocketed it. She noticed the napkin dampen as he touched it and thought that he had probably spilled some coffee on his fingers. "That's a good trait," she said. "Discretion, I mean."

"I think so."

"See you, Timothy." She turned her back before he could answer or keep her there with another soulful gaze or winning smile and left the café. The bus stop was a couple of blocks away, and in this kind of crowd she didn't want to risk orbing herself there or all the way back to work. If she happened across a quiet street or a private alley on the way, then she'd take the chance, but otherwise she'd just ride the bus and be a little late. It wasn't as if Cowan were going to kill her. He'd rant a little, and then he'd forget about it and be angry about something entirely different.

It would also take a lot more than one of Mr. Cowan's mindless rages to put a damper on her mood now. She had met exactly the kind of guy she had come to believe didn't exist, someone who could accept her for who she really was, someone she could talk to about anything, who would take her side without question and back her no matter what she did. Piper had Leo, Phoebe had Cole, and now—just maybe—she could have Timothy.

Obviously she still had to be cautious about him. She hadn't definitely admitted that she was a witch, much less let on that she was one of the Charmed Ones. That fact might make a difference to him. He might not want to be involved with someone whose life was constantly in danger. He might not even want to be involved with her at all. Maybe he had simply been a genuinely nice guy who wanted to buy her a cup of coffee for saving the boy—or let her buy him a cup of coffee—and then forget about her. After all, he hadn't so much as touched her, even when she'd slid the napkin to him, fully expecting him to brush his fingers against hers when he took it.

But she couldn't quite believe that either. He

had said he liked her. He had obviously meant more than just that he liked her; he had *like* liked her, as they'd said back in junior high. And he'd taken the phone number fast enough, tucking it into a pocket so he wouldn't lose it. No, she would be hearing from him, and soon.

But she hoped he meant what he said about discretion. She thought that she would try to keep Timothy a secret from her sisters, at least for a while. She needed something in her life that was just hers, that was outside the family circle. And she didn't want to bring him into the household, introduce him around, until she knew more about him and knew, without doubt, that he could be trusted with the knowledge of the Charmed Ones.

And that took a lot of trust.

Darryl Morris had barely made it to his desk when his phone rang. He snatched up the receiver. "Inspector Morris, SFPD," he said briskly.

"Darryl, it's Johnson. You're needed in the conference room."

"I just got here," Darryl replied. Monroe Johnson was another detective, junior to him, but he tended to get on Darryl's nerves. "I've been all over the city today, digging up files and talking to forensic examiners about these killings. I need some time to look through all this information."

"Bring it with you," Johnson said. "We'll need it."

"We?"

"Task force," Johnson told him.

Darryl hung up the phone. Police work wasn't what it had once been. Now everybody wanted instant results, and if that didn't happen, task forces were thrown together at the drop of a hat. The FBI would be waiting in the wings, and if the task force didn't have answers in a couple of days, the bureau would swoop in and take over.

He scooped up the dozens of file folders he had just deposited on his desk and wound his way through the police department's warren of cubicles to the conference room. There was a glass door, through which he figured Johnson must have seen him heading for his desk. He could see five detectives, three men and two women, sitting around a table in their shirt-sleeves, looking bored. He pushed the door open with his foot and went inside, where he dumped the files on the long wood grain metal table.

"Nice pants," Johnson said with a smirk as Darryl entered. He looked down and remembered that his suit pants were still filthy from the Gates place, stained and caked with mud. He'd tried to brush off as much as he could, but hadn't had time to change. Some of the other cops laughed nervously.

"Welcome to the task force," Lorraine Yee said, studiously ignoring Monroe Johnson. She flashed Darryl a smile that was stunning for its lack of sincerity. "Thanks for joining us, Darryl. We're it, we six. We can have some uniforms to help us do grunt work if we need it, but otherwise we're on our own. We all know why we're here, right?"

Darryl took a seat at the table, looking around at his fellow task force members.

"The wet killer," Leonard Scobie said. Leonard had been a detective longer than anybody. Though it couldn't be true, sometimes Darryl thought he'd been on the force since Prohibition—or maybe the gold rush.

"Is that what we're calling him?" Stephanie Payzant asked in surprise. The youngest member of the team was also, Darryl thought, the most attractive. Her brown hair was pulled back into a ponytail, and her men's cut shirt hung nicely on her athletic figure. "That's disgusting."

"It's what the *Chronicle*'s going to be calling him as of tomorrow's paper," Lorraine Yee replied. "Which means we've got to have some progress to report by the evening news tomorrow or the mayor's going to be very unhappy. Which means I'll be unhappy, which means . . . well, you know. Unhappiness all around."

A heavyset man sitting at the end of the table rubbed his forehead vigorously, as if trying to erase something he'd accidentally written there. "We would hate to cause you any unhappiness, Inspector Yee," Charlie Nordhoff said in a voice that sounded as if he gargled with ground glass every night. "You know we're just here to make your life pleasant and conflict-free."

"Thanks, Charlie," Lorraine said sharply. "Now shut up, all of you."

Monroe Johnson simply nodded and kept his mouth shut. Darryl did the same. Lorraine was famous for her lack of patience and tact. She could be the picture of calm when she was talking to a victim, but everything she bottled up then came out, in spades, with suspects and her fellow cops.

"We don't have to call him the wet killer if we don't want, but what I *do* want to call him is apprehended." She pointed to a corkboard against one wall on which someone had attached photos of the three dead women and their murder scenes and a large map of San Francisco, blue stickpins inserted at the murder locations. "What do we know about this guy?"

"We know it's a man," Johnson said.

"How do you know that?" Lorraine demanded.

"Well, chances are—"

She cut him off. "Chances aren't good enough. I didn't ask what we think, or speculate, or presume. I asked what we *know*."

Stephanie took up the challenge. "We know there are three women dead. We know that we haven't been able to identify the weapon, but it appears to be the same, or similar, in all three cases. We know there's been no physical evidence found at any of the crime scenes. That's about it, I think."

"Thank you," Lorraine Yee said, allowing herself a small smile. "That sums it up nicely. In other words, gentlemen and lady, what we know is not much, and what we don't know is voluminous. We need to turn that around. We need to know a lot and to make sure there's nothing we don't know. That's how we're going to catch this killer. There's no other way to do it, unless we happen to be standing on a street corner when he attacks his next vic. Everyone who thinks that's going to happen, raise your hands."

No hands were raised, but Lorraine waited for them just the same. Darryl had briefly considered raising his own, knowing he'd be ordered off the task force immediately. That would have been okay with him. He hated task forces with a passion. But he was also the only detective who had worked more than one of the scenes, since he had caught the first case as well as the most recent one, so he was the best resource they had right now. He had to stay, like it or not.

Besides, he really wanted to be there when they caught this guy.

Chapter
5

Phoebe sat cross-legged on her bed with a book in her lap because it was the best way to avoid having to talk to Piper or to deal with the fact that she really wasn't, for all intents and purposes, talking to Piper. Or Paige, for that matter, since she wasn't sure what she felt about Paige right now. Fortunately, Piper had spent most of the evening at P3, the nightclub she owned, making it easier to dodge her. Paige had seemed wrapped up in thoughts of her own and perhaps still a bit bent out of shape over the increasingly obvious fact that Phoebe and Piper disagreed over an issue they wouldn't talk to her about. They had crossed paths a few times during the evening, but conversation had been brief and superficial, with no attempts made to go to the heart of the matter facing them.

Phoebe was just realizing that she had scanned

the same page a dozen times without taking in a single word of what she had read when Leo orbed in. One look at his face told her that his trip hadn't met with notable success.

"Did you talk to her?" Phoebe asked, hopeful in spite of herself. She tucked a bookmark between the pages and set the book on a nightstand next to her bed. She had changed into blue plaid cotton pajama pants and a tank top long ago.

Leo nodded, his mouth set in a thin line, his face glum. "Found Aunt Agnes, talked to her." Phoebe had asked him—beleaguered him, really—to go find their deceased ancestor and find out precisely whom her letter had been meant for and if Paige had been the sister to whom it referred. With Piper out of the house, he had been slightly easier to convince, or he'd had no place to go to dodge her unending pleas. Even so, it had taken every ounce of persuasion she could muster, and it probably helped that Cole was off someplace, so that Leo didn't feel ganged up on. As a Whitelighter, Leo had died once, and he could visit the dead at will.

"And?"

"She's . . . not too communicative," Leo said. "At least not with me."

"What'd she say?"

"Verbatim?" he asked. "Or should I leave out the cursing? Which would make it a lot shorter, believe me."

Phoebe closed the book. "There was cursing?"

Leo plopped down on the end of her bed and rested his hands on his knees. "Entire ships full of sailors have used fewer curse words on six-month deployments."

That sounds like an exaggeration, Phoebe thought. *But he's got a military background, so I guess he'd know about such things.* Leo had been an army medic during World War II, killed in action during that conflict, actually. Because of his devotion to caring for others, he had become a Whitelighter.

"Tell me," Phoebe said. "You can leave out the cursing, but what about the rest of it?"

"There wasn't much 'rest,' I can assure you. Agnes was unfriendly when I got there. When I revealed that I'd come from Halliwell Manor, she went from being simply rude to outright antagonistic, just like that."

Phoebe noticed Leo offhandedly rub his jaw as he spoke. "She didn't . . . hit you, did she?"

"No," Leo said, then amended his own response. "Well, just once. And she's pretty frail, even for a ghost."

"She hit you?" Phoebe was stunned. "I guess her relationship with the rest of the family hasn't improved, even on the other side."

Leo nodded. "That was definitely the impression I had. She wouldn't give me the time of day. Not that, you know, the time of day means a lot to anyone there."

Phoebe slapped her knees in frustration. "There's just no way to make this easy, is there?"

"It's not an easy situation, Phoebe," Leo said. "If you're right, and I don't think you are, but if Paige is not who we think she is, that's going to be really tough on everyone. Piper loves her, and I think you do too. Can you imagine what it would do to both of you if she turned out to be a fake? Some kind of saboteur, working against the family from the inside?"

"I've thought about it. A little."

"And why would she have waited so long to make her move?"

"Trying to get us to trust her?" Phoebe said. "Waiting for the best time to wreak maximum havoc?"

Leo stifled a laugh. "Maximum havoc ought to be the motto around here," he said. "You could put it on a sampler by the front door. Paige wouldn't have to work hard to wreak some of that."

At the sound of the door opening downstairs, Phoebe tensed. It was probably just Piper or Cole, but there was always the chance that it was a demon or some other sort of creature coming to try to kill the sisters. Leo was right: Life at Halliwell Manor was far from calm.

"Lucy, I'm hooome!" Piper called out from the foyer.

"Piper," Leo announced, somewhat unnecessarily, since Phoebe hadn't genuinely believed it was Ricky Ricardo. "I should get down there."

Phoebe caught his knee as he started to rise. "Leo," she said, "thanks for what you did."

He shrugged. "I didn't really do anything."

"But you tried. You gave it a shot. That's more than anyone else has been willing to do."

"Believe me, if there's a way to bring peace to this household, I'm all for it." He stood and headed for the door.

Phoebe wasn't sure if she should follow, but then she heard another door open, and the distinctive sound of Paige's slippered feet going into the hall. "Hi, Piper," Paige said. "Have a good night?"

"It was fine," Piper said. "Another night of loud music, much dancing, much consumption of food and drink. Guess that's why they call it a nightclub."

Phoebe decided she should put in an appearance and opened her door. Leo had already descended the stairs and wrapped his arms around Piper. Paige stood at the top of the stairs in a baby doll nightie and her fuzzy slippers but looked just as wide awake as she had earlier in the evening. There was something different about her today, Phoebe remembered noticing, some kind of excitement that simmered just under the surface. Phoebe had thought that she was probably projecting because she was nervous about Paige, but looking at her now, she could still see it.

"My day was pretty good too," Paige told them. "I mean, you know, just work and that sale at Macy's that I didn't buy anything at. But it was still fun, I guess, looking at everything. Just looking, though."

She sounds nervous, Phoebe thought. *Like there's something she wants to tell us but is holding back.*

And if she's keeping secrets from us, are they the kind of secrets I'm starting to be afraid they might be?

They made uncomfortable small talk for another couple of minutes, and then everyone retired to a different direction.

Phoebe was just settling under her covers and reaching for the book again when there was a knock on her door. "Come on in," she called.

Piper opened the door hesitantly, then slipped inside and shut it behind herself. "Hi."

Phoebe waited for more, and when nothing came, she echoed Piper. "Hi."

Piper bobbed her head in the general direction of her room. "Leo, ah, told me what happened. What he did."

"I didn't mean for him to get hit," Phoebe said, hoping to head off any criticism on that score.

"No, I know. And I just wanted to let you know that, you know, I don't appreciate your using my husband that way."

Phoebe started to respond, but Piper kept talking, shutting her out. "But he's our

Whitelighter, and that's what he's supposed to do. And I do appreciate your coming up with the idea, and talking him into it, and trying to make sense out of this little problem we have here. That's what we should do, right? I mean, we're problem solvers. We work together. We get things done. That sounds like a résumé, but you know what I'm getting at."

"It didn't exactly accomplish much," Phoebe said. "She didn't even tell him if she wrote the letter or not."

"Well, that's true. But it was a valiant attempt. So we still have a problem, but thanks. For trying."

Phoebe wanted to say more, or to give her sister a hug, or something. Anything. But Piper just opened the door, let herself out, and shut it again. Phoebe was alone once more, with all her worries and fears about what the next day might bring.

But at least she had an older sister who loved her. No matter what.

You can't put a price on that, she thought.

Rosa Porfiro spent every evening inside a glass booth in a parking garage at one of the city's finest hotels, watching cars with names like BMW and Mercedes and Lamborghini, and sometimes a Hummer and an occasional old-fashioned Lincoln or Caddy go by. She sat on her stool and greeted the drivers, who were sometimes hired help and other times the owners themselves, and then, as the cars left, she checked their tickets and collected the money. Valets for the hotel also parked in the garage, and she knew each of them by name, of course, waved to them as they sped past in the expensive cars, cringed as they screeched brakes and squealed tires on the smooth oil-stained concrete floor.

And after her shift was over, Rosa waited for the Muni bus that would take her from Nob Hill to her street in the Sunset District, between Golden Gate Park and the zoo. The bus, she figured, probably cost more than any one of the cars that passed by her on a nightly basis, but of course it didn't belong to her, and its driver was not on her personal payroll. She paid a buck and she got a seat, and it went where it was supposed to go. Still, it was hard to imagine a better deal for someone like her. She'd never owned her own car and likely never would. She for sure would never drive a Jaguar or a Lexus. Even if she could, with parking so hard to find and expensive, the bus would still be her first choice.

Being wealthy, she often thought, would be fine. She could get used to it. But not being wealthy wasn't necessarily a bad thing. She and her husband, Rico, had a little house, and they had Patricio, their son, nine now and a handful, but a joy at the same time. Rico worked in construction, and someone in this city was always building, so there was always work to be had.

He liked being outdoors and working with his hands. Patricio went to school and then afternoon day care, and Rico was there to pick him up at the end of the day. Rosa was already on her way to work then, and Patricio was in bed by the time she got home at ten. But she saw him each morning, helped him get dressed and got him breakfast and walked him to school, and of course she spent every weekend with him. So she considered herself blessed, even though money was often tight and luxuries were few.

Patricio would be sound asleep now, but Rico would be up, sitting in the living room with the TV turned down low and a canvas in front of him. He painted seascapes, sights he saw when he worked on buildings near the waterfront. They were small, not much bigger than a postcard sometimes, and his cousin Lupe sold them at a flea market when she could, bringing in a few extra dollars. Rosa had found it surprising, at first, that such a big, strong man would paint such little paintings. But it was all about being good with his hands, he had explained to her. And a painting was just a structure, on a different scale. If it weren't built from the ground up, it all would fall apart.

Walking now from the bus stop three blocks from home, Rosa hurried her step, anxious to get there and see what he had worked on tonight. The neighborhood was quiet, enveloped in a dense fog. Almost every night was foggy here, so close to the ocean, even when Nob Hill was bright with stars and moonlight.

Rosa was thinking about home, about Rico's art and Patricio's slumbering form, when the fog turned solid in front of her. She collided with something and stepped back, too startled even to shout. "I'm sorry," she started to say after she'd had a second to collect herself. She figured she had run into someone, maybe one of the neighborhood's elderly people, walking a dog or just catching some night air. She couldn't see anyone, though. She hoped she hadn't knocked the person down. Her heart started to race. What if she had hurt someone?

Then the fog parted, and she saw a vague shape. Not an older person at all, she thought, but someone young. It was hard to tell for sure. The shape was indistinct, as if simply a shadow in the fog. The impression she had, though, was of someone young and menacing and coming toward her. She put up a hand, but the shadow person swatted it aside, hard. Now Rosa began to scream.

A wet hand clamped over her mouth, holding the scream inside. "No," a voice said. *Not a friendly voice*, she thought. *There is evil in that voice.* "I like the quiet, don't you?"

She wanted to struggle, to shake her head, to pray, to cry. But he held her in such a tight grip she couldn't move, couldn't draw her breath. Her eyes filled with tears as he held her, and

then she felt something sharp against her ribs
and a sudden hot pain. Rosa felt a sense of out-
rage. He had injured her! He had done something to her, and he had no right, no reason. . . .

Then she felt another pain, and another.
Liquid ran down her belly, and she knew it was
blood, knew that he was stabbing her, again and
again. The pain was hot, but Rosa was beginning
to feel cold, very cold, as if San Francisco's fog
itself had driven sharp-edged tendrils through
her soul.

Darryl Morris flashed his badge at the uniformed officer who held the perimeter, and the
young woman lifted the crime scene tape to let
him in. "Evening, sir," she said. She had very
straight white teeth and piled up under her hat,
a mass of coppery hair, strands of which had
escaped and hung down around her face. She
gave him a level gaze. "It's a messy one, sir."

"Aren't they all?" Darryl asked wearily.

"I wouldn't know, sir. I've been on the job
only three weeks. It's the worst I've seen."

Darryl started to respond but held his tongue.
If he had known at three weeks everything he
knew now, he would probably have quit the
police force and gone in for something safer,
more boring. *Lion tamer maybe*, he thought. *Or
that crocodile guy on TV. I could do that.* But he didn't
want to tell this young officer how he felt. She
had seen something horrible tonight, but she

could still smile, still do her job with efficiency
and a positive attitude. He didn't want to be the
one to break her spirit.

Forensics already had generators set up, running noisily and no doubt keeping the neighbors
awake, and bright lights on stanchions, bathing
the whole area in artificial daylight. Uniforms
were relegated to the outskirts, keeping the curious at bay and guarding the scene's perimeter.
Some were probably going door to door, checking to see if anyone had heard or seen the homicide. A couple of other task force members had
rolled up at about the same time as Darryl; he
saw Stephanie Payzant and Leonard Scobie
standing on the sidelines, taking notes, and
Lorraine Yee grilling one of the uniforms.

Darryl glanced toward the crowd of onlook-
ers. Some of them wore pajamas or robes, others
hastily pulled-on sweats or shorts, in spite of the
weather. A few were fully dressed, down to
overcoats against the night's chill. Darryl
intended to assign someone to get some pictures
of the crowd, and he even hoped to wander
among them, listening and looking and sniffing.
He could be there, Darryl knew. *Just watching us
work, playing innocent, getting his kicks by being so
close while we examine his bloody handiwork.*

Darryl had already decided on a couple of
things about the killer. He believed, just from the
initial report he'd heard, that this was the work of
the person who had already killed three times this

week. That meant they definitely had a serial killer
on the loose. Soon, maybe even tomorrow, the city
would figure it out and start to panic. If the task
force couldn't catch him fast, the FBI would come
in, and the chance that he, Darryl Morris, would
get to nail this bad guy would vanish.

And Darryl wanted to catch him. He wanted
it bad. He'd wanted it from the moment he laid
eyes on Gretchen Winter and Julia Tilton.

It was a male, most likely. Late twenties, early
thirties. After that, most of them were either
captured, or died, or matured out of the mad-
ness that drove them to kill. Almost certainly
Caucasian. Dysfunctional home life, father dead
or missing or just ineffectual, mother domineer-
ing, possibly abusive. Those things were all part
of the profile, and in spite of Lorraine Yee's dis-
like of profiles, it helped to keep them in mind.
A cop had to know what the odds were but not
to rely on them as definite. Darryl had to consider them likely aspects of his prey, while
remaining open to the possibility that his killer
could easily be an Eskimo woman in her sixties
with model parents. The ability to hold two con-
tradictory ideas at once: sure sign of a superior
mind. Sure sign of a San Francisco cop anyway.

When he looked at Rosa Porfiro, though, all
self-congratulatory thoughts vanished. She lay
on her back, her head cocked at an awkward
angle, eyes open and still fearful, even in death.
Her button-up sweater was open and stuck to

the tatters of her white hotel uniform polo shirt in some places, where blood had matted the two items together. There was a lot of blood, on her clothes and pooled beneath her from multiple wounds. He also noticed damp spots on her shoulder, near her neck.

"You're catching a lot of 'em these days," Ed Sweeney said. Sweeney, the coroner, was a small, round man with a tiny head that reminded Darryl of a grapefruit with eyes. In spite of the temperature, Sweeney was sweating. Darryl knew it was the man's only physical manifestation of the anger that built up inside him when he had to look at a murder victim. *A little round man who sweats on the coldest nights*, Darryl thought, *and with a mind like nobody's business*. Sweeney remembered everything he had ever heard, seen, or read and could recite it back verbatim. When it came to homicide, Darryl was very glad he had Ed Sweeney on his side.

"I wanted this one," Darryl said.

"Because of Tilton and the others?"

"That's right. Looks the same to you, too?"

Sweeney nodded. He pointed to the multiple stab wounds on Rosa's torso. "Same weapon as the other three. I still don't know for sure what it is. Nineteen wounds this time. Would have taken maybe three or four to be fatal, but this guy doesn't take chances."

"And her purse was with her?" Darryl asked, though he already knew the answer.

"Thirty-one dollars and fifty-two cents inside it," Sweeney answered. "A Visa, a driver's license, a library card, and several pictures of her family."

"Have they been notified?" That was the part of the job Darryl hated most, but that could be said of everyone who carried a badge. Telling someone that his wife, the mother of his children, had been murdered left scars that never healed. Darryl had nightmares about it sometimes, even when he hadn't had to do it in days or weeks.

"A uniform went to do it right away," Sweeney said. "Sanchez, I think it was. Victim lives just a couple of blocks from here."

That meant, Darryl knew, that the family could come over to the scene if Sanchez wasn't able to keep them at home. This wasn't something they should see, and it would only interfere with the investigation. The family's feelings were important, but so was stopping this guy before he could do this to another family, and another. The fact that Rosa Porfiro's people were close by just added one more layer of urgency to his job.

Darryl swallowed hard and bent over Rosa's body. "Come on, then," he said to Sweeney. "Let's get this over with."

Chapter

6

Piper went downstairs and into the kitchen to make some breakfast. When she got there, Phoebe and Paige were already seated at the table, pointedly not looking at or talking to each other. Tension was as thick as the fog outside. Coffee was brewed, so Piper poured herself a cup and opened the refrigerator to look for some fresh fruit. There was none. She gave up on that, then remembered that there had been some blueberry muffins the day before.

"Has anybody seen the muffins?" she asked of no one in particular.

"Phoebe had the last one," Paige declared around a mouthful of toast. "And before you ask, this is the last of the bread, so no toast either."

Piper shot them both an anguished glare. Phoebe met her eyes only briefly, but her gaze was more defiant than sorry. "There's a little bit of cereal," she said. "But you'll have to eat it dry. I put the last of the milk in my coffee."

"Doesn't anyone in this house remember where the grocery store is?" Piper moaned. "And before anyone complains, I include myself in that."

"I guess we've just all been busy," Paige said. "What with working and chasing demons and everything."

As far as Piper could remember, last night Phoebe and Paige both had spent the whole evening sitting around the house not talking to each other. But to point that out would just be to exacerbate an already uncomfortable situation, so she left it alone.

"Well, maybe I'll just get something to eat on my way," Piper said. She had already dressed in casual black pants and a purple ribbed top. "I have a couple of early appointments with suppliers at P3, so I've got to get going." This much was true; she had a nine o'clock and then a ten-thirty, both with suppliers who'd be taking inventory of her stock and then sitting down with her to take orders. It would be a busy morning, no question.

Phoebe picked up her mug and carried it to the sink. "I have a job interview, so I need to head out too."

"Oh, that's great, Phebes," Paige said brightly. "With who?"

"A small bookstore chain with its head office here in the city," Phoebe said. "It's not a great job, a receptionist position, but it'd bring in some money, and I wouldn't mind being able to help pay for those groceries again, still, I don't have a very good feeling about the interview."

"Why not?" Piper inquired.

Phoebe hesitated, as if unsure how much she wanted to say. "Just . . . I haven't been sleeping that well, lately."

That was a lie, or at the very least a half-truth, but Piper let it go. Phoebe had a lot more on her mind than just sleeping problems.

"Well, good luck with it," Paige told her. "Sounds like fun, and I'm sure you'll do just great." She seemed to be making a genuine attempt to carve through the iceberg of tension that filled the room. Piper watched Phoebe carefully, curious about what response she might make. For a moment Phoebe's eyes softened, and she looked at Paige as she would the trusted sister she once was. *And will be again*, Piper thought. But then Phoebe's eyes hardened, and her lips pressed together, making her mouth a narrow line. She had remembered that she wasn't sure if she trusted Paige, Piper knew. Phoebe turned her gaze on Piper, and the eyes were just as hard. *O-kay*, Piper thought, *still ticked at me, too.*

Well, that was just fine. She wasn't all that happy with Phoebe either and wouldn't be until she started cutting Paige some slack over that stupid letter. Especially now that she'd used up the last of the muffins and milk.

"All right then," Piper said, anxious to get away before she said something she'd regret later. "Bye!"

She headed back upstairs to brush her teeth and say good-bye to Leo.

Even when Mr. Cowan was in a good mood—and that was rare—Paige's job was stressful. People didn't make use of Social Services when their lives were running smoothly, only when they were at some kind of crisis point. Nasty child custody disputes, deadbeat or missing parents, abusive relationships, homelessness: Those were the kinds of issues that filled Paige's working day. There were times when it all got to be too much, and Paige was glad that she had the extra outlet of being able to use her witchy powers and kick demon butt once in a while, if only to blow off a little steam.

Today, for instance, she had spent much of the morning on the phone with a succession of police departments and social workers in different states, trying to track down a so-called mother who had decided to "find herself" by following a second-rate rock 'n' roll band on its tour of dives and roadhouses of the northern plains. This woman had quit her job and vanished with no notice, leaving Jarrod Boone, her husband, with three kids under seven, a cleaned-out bank account, and a note asking him to watch the kids and not try to find her.

Mr. Boone had done his best with the first part but refused to go along with the second. With just his own income, he could barely cover the child care costs for the kids while he went to work. That didn't leave much for rent, food, and the other necessities of life, which her income and their savings had helped pay for. He thought his kids needed a mother, but more important, he didn't want them to find themselves living in a car or a shelter, so he wanted his wife found, and their savings returned, at the very least. The police wouldn't touch the case, and he couldn't afford a private detective. So he had come to Social Services instead.

The runaround Paige got on the phone was annoying. She couldn't understand why people wouldn't just be straight with her. If a police officer in Podunk, Michigan, didn't want to take the time to see if the former Mrs. Boone was registered at any of the motels there, he could just say so instead of transferring Paige to someone else, who would in turn transfer her to yet another person, before she was finally cut off altogether. Several times she nearly lost her patience, but she tried to keep in mind that doing so wouldn't actually get her anywhere. *More flies with honey, and all that,* she thought.

Anyway, to keep herself sane, she thought about Timothy and the exceedingly pleasant cup

of coffee they'd shared the day before at Union
Square. Normally she would have been all over
telling Piper and Phoebe about something like
that, but however one wanted to describe life at
witch central these days, *normal* wasn't a word
that came to mind. The fact that she wasn't talking about him, though, didn't mean she wasn't
thinking about him. Quite the contrary. When
her phone calls got to be too exasperating, she
simply recalled the sound of his laugh, so full of
enthusiasm that she couldn't help joining in or
the way he looked at her with such admiration
when he talked about how she'd helped the little
boy.

Paige had just hung up after yet another useless phone call—there was no Podunk, Michigan,
as it happened, but there was a Pompeii, and the
authorities there were most unhelpful—when
her line rang. Hoping against hope that one of
her many inquiries had finally reached someone
who cared, she snatched up the receiver.

"Paige Matthews, Social Services," she said
cheerfully.

"That's what I like to hear," a male voice said,
"someone who's happy in her work." Before she
could answer, he went on. "This is Timothy,
Paige. I don't know if you remember me—"

"Of course I remember you, Timothy. Union
Square, floating coffee cup. How could I forget?"

"I'm glad to hear that," he said. "You sound
like you're having a better day than yesterday."

Paige thought that over for a moment. "I don't know about that," she said finally. "It's actually a pretty lousy day overall. But I try not to let people who call me here know that. Compared with most of them, I have a peachy life."

"That's probably true. I don't mean to take you away from your work or anything. I was just thinking about you and wanted to check in."

Paige thought she could almost feel her heart swelling at those words. "I've been thinking about you too, Timothy," she told him.

"Just good things, I hope."

"Of course good things."

"Great," he said, sounding genuinely pleased. "So, saved any little kids today?"

"I'm trying to save three," she replied. "From the worst enemy of all—poverty."

"Wow," he said, his tone one of admiration, almost awe. "What a great job. And you're the perfect person for it. When I saw that you were a witch, I was hoping that you were one of the good ones and that saving the kid wasn't just some kind of fluke. But it's obvious that it wasn't. You really do care about helping people."

"Yeah, I guess I do," Paige said. She let her eyes wander around her glass-walled cubicle.

"I knew you were one of the good ones," he said.

She felt herself blushing a little, even with no one there to see her. "Thanks. I guess you are too."

"That's right," Timothy replied. "From way back. Ramona Frey, one of my ancestors, used to work with another witch, whose name was . . . something like Halloween, I remember thinking." Paige felt her heart skip a beat when he said that, but she kept quiet and let him continue. "No, Halliwell. Agnes Halliwell. Together the two of them vanquished just about every demon west of the Mississippi, the way my mom used to tell it."

"Agnes Halliwell?" Paige repeated. "I don't think I've heard that name."

"But you've heard about the Halliwells? The Charmed Ones?"

She felt torn. If she lied to him now, it would be a terrible way to start a relationship—if, in fact, he had any interest in a relationship. But she had learned, the hard way, that the sisters had to be constantly on their guard. The Charmed Ones had too many enemies for her to reveal her true identity too lightly, especially to someone who might know what it meant.

But the whole point of knowing Timothy is that I want a relationship, she decided. *And sometimes what I want has to count.*

"I've heard of them," she told him. She almost had to force the words out. "In fact, I am a Halliwell, kind of."

She could hear the surprise in his intake of breath. "I thought you were a Matthews," he said.

"I am," she replied. "Same mother as the two Halliwell sisters, different father."

"So you're one of the Charmed Ones? That's amazing. No wonder I felt such a vibration of good coming off you."

Paige laughed. "Well, sometimes I can be bad."

"I bet," Timothy said. "But not in the way I'm talking about."

"It was touch and go for a while there," she said, remembering the struggle she'd had when she first found out she was a witch. The Source had wanted to pull her to the side of evil. Since Prue had died, that would have permanently limited the Power of Three. And she had very nearly gone along with it.

"So you're a Charmed One," Timothy said again, "and you've never heard of Agnes Halliwell?"

"Should I have?"

Timothy hesitated for a long moment. "Paige," he said at length, "I think you can tell I like you, and I want only the best of everything for you. So it's difficult for me to tell you this. But I think you need to know who Agnes is. And there's something else you need to know."

"What is it, Timothy?" she demanded. "You're kind of freaking me out here."

"I can't tell it to you," he replied. "You need to learn it for yourself. And the only way to do that is to go into your sister Phoebe's room when there's no one home. She has a letter, in her nightstand. You need to read it."

"But . . . that's snooping!" Paige exclaimed. "She'd kill me. And . . . it's wrong. And she'd kill me."

"She doesn't have to know," he said. "I don't want to stir anything up, Paige, but she's keeping a secret from you, and you deserve to know about it. You *need* to know about it."

Paige swallowed, hard. She had been feeling as if Phoebe and Piper were keeping something from her, there was no denying that. Phoebe had been especially distant, almost as if Paige had offended her in some way. Piper had been different. Paige had the distinct sense that she was mad at Phoebe, while Phoebe was just plain mad. "Can I ask you something, Timothy?"

"Sure, Paige. Anything."

"If it's a secret, how do you know about it?"

He chuckled, and the sound relaxed her a little. *Not everything in life is awful,* she thought, *as long as there's someone whose laugh does that to me.* "We all have powers, Paige," he told her. "I guess knowing about stuff like that is one of mine."

They made small talk for another couple of minutes, and then Paige reluctantly said goodbye and hung up. It was almost lunchtime, and she had every intention of taking his advice to heart.

Phoebe had flat-out lied to her sisters, and she

hated the way that made her feel. She had a job interview today—that much was true—but it wasn't until early afternoon. She had simply wanted to get away from the house, away from the pressure she could feel building up inside it like water boiling in a covered pot, until at some point it had to be released or explode.

So she had made the interview sound as if it were earlier in the day, and then she'd gotten into her midnight blue Jeep and gone for a drive. She headed south, out of the city, since San Francisco driving was not something one could do without focus, and Phoebe wanted to clear her mind, give it space to wander and see if she could make sense of the whole unpleasant situation. She took the 280 freeway out of town, past San Andreas Lake and down the peninsula through oak-dotted grassy hills. The freeway led her out of the fog and, she hoped, out of the fog of uncertainty that surrounded her. The only person she wished she'd been able to bring along was Cole because he was a great sounding board for even her craziest ideas. But he was busily applying the skills he had learned in law school and the district attorney's office, helping Leo and Piper investigate some murders they were thinking might somehow tie in to the supernatural. He had promised to meet her after her interview, though.

She had every intention of turning around before she reached the heart of Silicon Valley, the

area from Palo Alto and beyond where fortunes
had been won and lost so often—frequently by
the same people, again and again—over the past
couple of decades. She'd half expected, when
she found herself down that way during the
height of the dot-com boom, that she'd find the
road blocked by a tollgate, where mere common-
ers would have to pony up five or ten thousand
dollars just to be admitted into the rarefied air of
the valley. She had been sorry when the boom
ended and regular folks lost their jobs, but at the
same time it didn't disturb her that real estate
prices might one day reach normal proportions
again and those same regular folks might once
more be able to buy homes in the Bay Area.

But the valley would be farther out of town
than Phoebe wanted to go today, too far to let
her comfortably get back in time for her interview. She didn't want to find herself rushing and
frantic at the last minute. She pulled off the freeway at Woodside, drove down a short, forested,
winding stretch of road to where she knew there
was a wood frame marketplace, and stopped
long enough to get a veggie sandwich and a cold
Snapple for lunch. She ate it sitting at a table outdoors in the sun, which she hadn't seen much of
in San Francisco the past few foggy days. She
hadn't made any progress in her overall dilemma,
which involved trying to figure out how to
know if Aunt Agnes's letter was about Paige or
not, but she felt a little better, nonetheless. The

drive and the lovely weather on the peninsula
had helped clear some of the cobwebs from her
head.

When Phoebe made it back to San Francisco
for her interview, she found that she was actually looking forward to it, that the brief trip out
of town had changed her mood substantially. Of
course parking in the city could always change it
back. She circled the block twice, then expanded
her search. Finally, three blocks away from the
office of the bookstore chain, she found a spot
and squeezed the Jeep into it.

She had cut the timing a little closer than she
was comfortable with. She hurried down the
sidewalk and almost tripped over a copper
bracelet she hadn't seen before she stepped on it.
Pausing, she bent over and picked it up, intending to set it against the wall, where it would be
out of the way but still obvious if its owner came
back to look for it.

That was when the vision hit, taking her
breath away with its sudden, violent impact. She
saw a dark street, damp with fog, a young
woman in some kind of uniform, and a malevo-
lent presence on the prowl, moving in for the
kill. Then it went away, and Phoebe was alone
on the fog-shrouded sidewalk again, her knees
rubbery.

Shaken, Phoebe leaned against a parking
meter. She tried to make sense of the premonition. It was definitely night, so the woman wasn't

in imminent danger. There might still be time to track her down and save her from the stalking would-be killer. She didn't know if this related in any way to the case that Piper, Leo, and Cole were working on, but if it did, the supernatural aspect had just been confirmed.

But she couldn't recognize the location. It was just a San Francisco street like a hundred others, with a thick smudge of fog obscuring any details that might have helped clarify it. She focused on the woman instead, trying to recall any details that might help identify her. There was obviously the uniform; even though Phoebe didn't recognize it, if she could determine where it was from, that would be a major step in finding her. The top had been a dark blue peasant-style blouse with gold thread around the neckline and sleeves, and the skirt red with blue patterns that echoed the blouse. She'd worn plain, comfortable black flats with it, and Phoebe remembered that there were whitish stains on the shoes. A waitress, most likely. The stains were from spilled food—clam chowder, maybe, or tartar sauce. *So a seafood place?* she thought. *Maybe.*

That, given that San Francisco was surrounded on three sides by water, didn't narrow it down much. Phoebe didn't have much sense of the woman herself; she had thick dark hair and eyes and olive skin, so possibly Latina or Middle Eastern. Mid-twenties, at a guess.

So many unknowns, though. Phoebe found

herself wishing she could demand more information, but her power didn't work that way. She took what she was given and tried to save the innocent when she could. One thing was sure: She wasn't going to do any good standing here. She released the parking meter and continued on toward her interview.

Chapter

7

This time Paige didn't bother with public transportation. She found some privacy in the women's room of the Social Services office and orbed straight home, arriving in the foyer. For a moment she wondered how she'd explain why she was home in the middle of the day if there was anyone here. Even though she was pretty sure Piper would still be at work, Phoebe had only an interview, and that could well be over. Then there were Leo and Cole, whose comings and goings were unpredictable at best. Paige opened the front door and then slammed it behind her. "It's just me!" she shouted up the stairs. "Anyone home?"

When there was no answer, she started up the stairs, thinking, *I've seen this movie. I get into her room with no problem, but just when I've found what I'm looking for, someone discovers me there. Ugly*

*scene ensues; feelings are hurt; words are spoken.
Come to think of it, I've always hated that movie.*

She stopped in front of Phoebe's door. *I
shouldn't be here*, she told herself. *I should just turn
around and leave. Go back to work. Forget what
Timothy said. What does he know anyway? What
could he possibly know about us?*

But she couldn't bring herself to do it. She
knocked on the door, twice softly, then harder.
Just in case. Knocking on a sister's door? What
could be more innocent?

Her knocks raised no response, so she tried
the knob. Unlocked. She went inside and closed
the door quickly behind herself, her heart trip-
hammering with anxiety.

Phoebe's room looked the way it always did:
yellow-and-white striped wallpaper, fresh flow-
ers everywhere, lace curtains filtering the sunlight that washed through the big window. Paige
could see nothing that appeared to be a hidden
spy camera or a listening device. *Of course*, she
reasoned, *if there was a hidden camera and I could
see it right away, it wouldn't be very hidden.* She
couldn't quite imagine that her sister was trying
to catch her being underhanded; that would be
pretty underhanded in itself. Still, she couldn't
shake the feeling that there was something
wrong about this whole situation, even beyond
the obvious.

*I shouldn't be here I shouldn't be here I shouldn't
be here . . .* Paige repeated it to herself like a

mantra as she crossed the floor. She stopped when she stepped on a particularly squeaky board, as if there were anyone home to hear her, and then continued toward the nightstand, looming in her imagination the way the Golden Gate Bridge did over the mouth of the bay. When she finally reached her destination, Paige tugged open the drawer.

There, lying on top of some hair clips and a bottle of hand lotion, was an envelope.

It looked old, obviously predating her birth by ages. What it might have to do with her, Paige had no idea. But Timothy had said that Agnes Halliwell had been friends with one of his ancestors, so it made sense that if she was involved, whatever this was about had happened long ago.

Part of her—a big part, really—wanted to put the envelope down and walk away. She found that she was actually pleased by how tempting the idea was. She could prove, if only to herself, that she was no snoop, that she was a bigger person than that. Of course, the only person she'd ever be able to tell would be Timothy, and since he'd been the one urging her on in the first place, he probably wouldn't be all that impressed.

Unless this is some kind of test, she thought. *Maybe he wants me to come back and tell him I couldn't go through with it. Then he'll give me a big hug and congratulate me on being accepted into some superspecial witch club, and I'll get the secret handshake and the membership card and everything.*

It took only a few seconds to realize how unlikely that was, though. She sat on the edge of Phoebe's bed and opened the envelope. Inside, she found a letter on paper that was so old and brittle she was afraid it would break apart in her hands like late-autumn leaves. Carefully unfolding it, she found writing in ink that had browned against the aging paper, almost becoming the same color. Between that and the scratchy handwriting, made, it appeared, at least a hundred years ago with a crow quill pen, she could barely read it.

But after she had stared at it for a little while, it began to come clear for her. The letter was a warning, it seemed, addressed to "Charmed Ones," whom, she believed, had been known of but who hadn't actually existed in those days. As she read further, she felt a horrific sensation. Her stomach churned, her throat almost seemed to close off, and she couldn't catch her breath.

"A sister shall die, and a new one shall take her place," she read. "But the new witch is no ally, mark me well. A traitor she is, and once entrusted by the family, this devil shall endanger the Power of Three."

She means me, Paige thought. *It couldn't be anyone else.*

And Phoebe believes her.

That was what all the tension had been about, Paige realized. Phoebe had found this letter somewhere and believed every word of Agnes's warning. Somehow, Timothy knew about it, and that was why he had sent Paige here: because Phoebe, who was her sister and was supposed to love her and trust her, couldn't even bring herself to confront Paige with her suspicions.

Piper probably knew too, Paige understood. The whole household had been on edge the last couple of days. Maybe they'd been arguing about when to tell her, or how, or the best way to test her. *She* knew she wasn't a traitor, but she didn't know how she could prove that. If her sisters wanted to believe the worst, there probably wasn't much she could do about it.

Anyway, if the traitor's goal was to endanger the Power of Three, as the letter said, it seemed that goal had already been achieved. Sisters who couldn't talk to one another about something as relatively simple as an old letter from a long-dead relative certainly wouldn't be able to put their lives in one another's hands on the field of battle. *Would Phoebe trust me to have her back in a fight against some nasty demon with a hunger for witches?* she wondered.

For that matter, after this would I trust her? Maybe she's just waiting for a good opportunity to take me out, so she doesn't have to worry about my betraying her anymore.

A tear rolled off Paige's cheek and splashed onto the paper, smearing the ink a little. Realizing she was in danger of revealing that she'd been in

Phoebe's room, she sniffed, folded up the letter, stuck it back in its envelope, and replaced the envelope in the drawer. She left Phoebe's room as quickly as she could, pausing just long enough to snatch a tissue from a box on the dresser. In the hall she closed Phoebe's door and then blew her nose.

She hadn't been caught. She'd pulled off her little breaking-and-entering routine without a hitch.

But she couldn't help feeling that it might have been better if someone had been there to stop her. Now she had to go back to work knowing that her entire life had just been turned upside down.

Lorraine Yee punctuated her own speech by thunking her blunt fingernail against the corkboard whenever she pointed to one of the pictures or the map. A new photo had joined the three already there when the task force had been formed, and Darryl knew if they didn't come up with some answers in a hurry, there would be more. This killer wasn't slowing down, wasn't getting nervous or taking extra care. He seemed to believe he was invulnerable and so killed with perfect abandon. The knowledge tugged at him, made him wish he were out on the street instead of sitting in this stuffy conference room, breathing in stale air, sweat, and the stink of coffee left in the pot too long.

"Gretchen Winter," Lorraine said, poking at her portrait. She moved to the next one. "Sharlene Wells. Julia Tilton. And now Rosa Porfiro." She stopped by that one's picture, a five-by-seven print made of a shot taken the night before, after the woman had met her violent end. "We have a young African-American woman, Sharlene. Two Caucasian women, Gretchen Winter, in her forties, and Julia Tilton, barely twenty. And Rosa Porfiro, a Latina who would have been thirty-nine next week. Winter killed in Potrero Hill, Wells in Cow Hollow, Tilton in Nob Hill, Porfiro in the Sunset." She scanned the faces of the task force members, locking on to the eyes of each one for what Darryl considered an uncomfortably long time. That, he supposed, was the point. Lorraine didn't want them comfortable. She wanted them out on the edge, where they'd be more likely to come up with the intuitive leaps that separated the great detectives from the plodders. Both kinds could close cases, but this case wasn't looking like one for the plodders.

"What, other than the way they died, do these women have in common?" she asked. "The answer to that question may be our best chance to find their killer. Unless the killings are completely random, crimes of opportunity and nothing more, there has to be some linking element. It's not age, race, or income level. Gender, yes—they're all women. And I shouldn't have to remind you, lady and gentlemen, that San Francisco is full of women. I don't want to see any more of them up on this board."

Lorraine's idea was sound, Darryl knew. Normally the victims of a serial killer were connected in some way. They shared some physical characteristic, or they all frequented some business where the killer had come into contact with them, or they shared some lifestyle that made them targets. But Darryl knew something that Lorraine Yee and the other cops on the task force didn't and that something threw a monkey wrench into all "normal" theories of criminal behavior.

Since becoming acquainted with the Halliwells, as much as he had wanted to deny it at first, Darryl knew about witchcraft and about the warlocks and demons who preyed on both witches and humans. He knew there was a whole otherworldly side to life that occasionally impacted on the civilian world and that police departments had to deal with the repercussions of such events without ever knowing what was really going on. It had occurred to him many times that the cops would have had a better handle on things, and therefore been able to keep the populace safer, if they all had known what he did.

At the same time, he understood that good witches, and the Charmed Ones in particular, would quite likely become targets for humans who couldn't handle the news that their world was more complicated than they had thought. The Charmed Ones were targeted enough as it was by those same warlocks and demons, and if humans got into the act, the Halliwells might one day lose the battle. Darryl knew that a world without Charmed Ones would be infinitely more dangerous than a world in which witchcraft remained a secret. So he kept his mouth shut and tried to apply his knowledge quietly when he could.

Leo had called Darryl with some questions on the murders, so Darryl knew that he and Piper already believed there was a supernatural element to these killings. They were looking into it on their own, and he welcomed the help. Anything to bring the murderer to justice, of one kind or another. If they were right, all the task forces the city could muster wouldn't help as much as their powers would.

In the meantime he and these other dedicated cops would keep working whatever slim leads they could find the old-fashioned way, through footwork and the sweat of human labor.

"Darryl," Lorraine said impatiently, and he realized he hadn't heard her call on him the first time, lost as he was in his own thoughts. "You still with us?"

"Yes, sorry, Lorraine," he said, shaking his head to clear it. "What is it?"

"You've done more background work than

the rest of us on this case so far. You pulled all
the files, dug into the history of these women a
bit. Can you point the way to any connections
we're missing?"

He had been looking for exactly that answer
and so far had come up blank. "I'm afraid it's
pretty much as you described it. Different
socioeconomic levels, different neighborhoods,
different races. I haven't been able to nail down
anything specific. You know, maybe they all buy
coffee from the same place or take Sunday walks
in the park at the same time, something like that.
We could canvass their friends and relatives
again, try to get a better picture of their day-to-
day lives. But so far nothing's turned up."

"That's everybody's assignment for today
then," Lorraine told them. She glanced over her
shoulder at the board again and waved a hand
at the photos. "Get to know these ladies, inside
and out. Something connects them. We need to
know what it is."

Darryl thought she was about to dismiss
them when there was a tap at the door and a
uniformed officer stepped in. Lorraine met him
near the doorway, and they spoke in hushed
tones for a moment. Then the officer left, and
Lorraine faced the group, sadness evident on her
face. "There's another body," she said quietly.
"Let's get to work."

Phoebe sat in a crowded office across from

Michael Langdon, the president of the book chain. He was a lean, wild-eyed man with a thick mop of curly dark hair, small glasses, and a full beard, who was dressed in a blue work shirt and worn jeans. His office was packed with books, stacks of them that looked as if they would be a safety hazard during an earthquake. There were recent hardcovers that she recognized, paperbacks without cover art, which he had explained were advance reading copies publishers sent for booksellers and reviewers to read before they arrived in stores, and old books of every size and description, caked in dust, that looked as if they'd been part of the office forever. Phoebe had been to a couple of this chain's stores in different parts of the city, and they had always been clean and orderly, so she was astonished at the difference in the head office.

She wanted to solve the mystery of the uniformed woman in danger, but she figured the interview would delay that for only an hour at the most, and there were still many hours to go before dark. And a job of course would bring with it a whole host of benefits, not least of which was a steady paycheck. Even though Grams had left them the house free and clear, there was a constant outflow of money, and she felt bad letting Piper and Paige carry that weight all by themselves.

"Do you read a lot, Phoebe?" Langdon inquired. The interview had so far skittered from one subject to another without any seeming pattern. She thought maybe the man didn't do a lot of interviewing.

"Well, I try to," she replied. "I'm pretty busy, though." She realized that sounded lame, since he knew she was currently unemployed, and of course she couldn't tell him about the witch stuff. So what kept her too busy to read, he might wonder, watching reality TV and eating bonbons?

He didn't go there, however. "When you do find the time, what do you enjoy?"

She couldn't even remember the name of the book she had tried to read the other night, while waiting for Leo to report back. "You know, there's fiction. And then also . . . um . . . nonfiction." She had to do better than that, but she was distracted by her own thoughts and by the urgency of her premonition. She gave it another try. "I like books that take me away from my daily problems, to someplace new and interesting."

"Yes," Langdon said, nodding. She couldn't tell if she was impressing him or terrifying him. He just kind of nodded to himself, and his expression never changed. She suspected that he was every bit as distracted as she was, as if this interview were just a heinous chore he wanted to put behind him as quickly as possible. He wasn't asking follow-up questions, just jumping to the next thing that came into his mind.

"The job, you know, is a front-desk position.

You'd be answering phones, setting appointments with publishers' reps, and also taking and processing stock orders from our various stores. Those orders come in over the phone, by fax, and online. You get the orders organized and turned in to the warehouse crew, and then once they've pulled the stock, you report back to the stores to let them know what they need to get from some other source."

"I would have thought that would all be computerized," Phoebe commented. "Inventory, I mean."

"You'd think so, wouldn't you?" Langdon replied. "Not entirely, though. Not yet. We still like to let people make some of those decisions for themselves, instead of machines. Call us antiques, but we've been in business since 1846, and sometimes we like doing things the way they've always been done."

She didn't want to point out that they wouldn't have had phones, faxes, or the Internet in 1846, so she just nodded, kept her mouth shut, and waited for the next question.

"Do you have flexibility in your schedule?" he asked her. This was what she'd been waiting for; she didn't want a job that would tie her to a desk eight hours a day, five days a week, because the life of a Charmed One didn't fall into such a neat schedule. Paige tried to maintain her job in spite of the demands of her other life, but the two frequently came into conflict.

"Because," he continued, "there are times, especially as we get closer to the holiday season, when we keep the office open late and on weekends. From Thanksgiving through Christmas Eve it sometimes seems like we never get out of here."

Oh, she thought, disappointed. *Flexibility in the wrong direction.* That wouldn't work at all. What would she tell her sisters? "Sorry, you guys are on your own for this battle. I've got to make sure the Carmel store has enough copies of the new Stephen King."

This wasn't looking promising at all, she knew. Too bad. It'd be fun to work around books, even if most of the books were back in the warehouse while she would be out in the lobby with the phones and a computer.

But her sisters and their calling had to come first.

That must mean something, she thought. *When I'm not dwelling on that letter, my subconscious mind still trusts them.*

Even if nothing else came out of the interview, that much was good to know.

Chapter

8

"Piper!"

"Gaaah!" Piper had to stifle a startled scream. She had just carried a clipboard back into the nightclub's wine cellar and was kneeling on the floor, counting cases of a popular chardonnay when Leo had orbed in, unnoticed until he spoke. "You nearly gave me a heart attack," she said, clipping her words short. In spite of her momentary fright, though, he was still her guy. She stood and went to him, to draw him into her arms. "And you shouldn't even be in here. What if Max comes in?"

Max worked for the distributor that supplied the wine. She had left him at the bar, counting the bottles there, but there was always the chance that he'd think of something he needed to look at in the cellar.

"Sorry, Piper," Leo said, kissing her forehead.

"I'll keep it short, but I really think you should ditch Max and come with me."

"I can't ditch Max," Piper told him. "As much as I love hanging out with you, and I'm sure you're doing something very important, I have to keep this club running. We do still need to have some income, you know. P3 is the best source we have. I can't just blow it off."

She started to turn back to her count, but Leo took her by the shoulders and stared into her eyes. *This is serious*, she realized. He had his you've-got-to-listen-to-me-now face on, and that wasn't something Leo trotted out without good reason. "Okay, what?" she asked.

Leo nodded toward the ceiling. She knew he didn't mean upstairs this time. "I've been visiting some Halliwells," he told her, "asking about good old Aunt Agnes."

"Did any of them hit you?"

"Not this time," he said with the ghost of a smile. "But they did tell me a story. And not the happy kind."

"Tell me," she said. "And quick, before Max wonders why it's taking so long to count a few cases of wine."

"If you'll stop interrupting, Piper, that was exactly what I had in mind," her husband said. She mimed zipping her lip and let him continue. "The family, back during Agnes's time, became aware of a warlock who was killing innocents. This is a hundred years ago, give or take. Of course, your ancestors objected and tried to find out who the warlock was, to stop him."

"Of course," Piper said, then remembered she was zipped. She let Leo go on.

"They narrowed it down to a single suspect. But Aunt Agnes, never everybody's favorite to begin with, thanks to her foul temper and general contrariness, said that their suspect couldn't be the right guy. He was, she claimed, her long-lost brother, and he would never hurt a fly that didn't deserve it. She protected him from the rest of the family as long as she could. The whole time the body count was going up. People were disappearing from all over San Francisco, and even though only a few bodies ever showed up, the witches knew that someone was murdering the missing people. And they were pretty sure they knew who it was."

"We're talking about a lot of people?" Piper inquired.

"A lot," Leo answered. "Finally, after alienating the whole family and creating hard feelings that still haven't passed, Agnes realized her mistake. He had tricked her into thinking he was an estranged brother, but he wasn't really. She told the family about her mistake but still refused to tell them where the fake brother was hidden. Then she went up against the warlock herself. By then he had become very powerful; somehow, he seemed to have been drawing power from the murders, so the more people he killed, the stronger he grew. The battle, according to the family members I talked to, must have been terrible. Agnes finally won, even though the injuries she took eventually killed her, too. She vanquished the warlock, and the killings stopped."

"So Great-Great-Some random number of greats-Aunt Agnes died a hero," Piper commented. "That's unexpected, considering what Phoebe found in the *Book of Shadows*. Or didn't find."

"A hero, but only in the sense that she solved a problem she had been partially responsible for creating," Leo said. "Remember, if she hadn't stood in the way in the first place, the family would have vanquished him that much sooner, and a lot of lives would have been saved."

Before she could respond, she heard the deep bass voice of Max Cooper, calling from the other room, "Piper? You in here?"

Piper glanced at Leo, already orbing out. "Yes," she replied when he was gone.

Max stuck his head around the cellar door. He was a handsome man who sang opera as a hobby, performing at various venues around town. She loved to hear him talk, just to enjoy the richness of his voice. "I was beginning to think you'd started sampling."

"No such luck," she told him. "I'm almost done. How about you?"

"Ready to write an order," he said. "All I

need is you, pretty lady." In addition to singing, Piper knew, Max's other hobby was being an incorrigible flirt. She knew he wasn't serious and didn't mind the attention, though she thought it would be interesting if he knew that her husband was hovering nearby, out of sight.

"Get the paperwork started, and I'll meet you at the bar," Piper said. "I just need a couple of minutes."

"I'll be counting the seconds," he said with a wink. As his footsteps faded toward the bar, Piper closed the cellar door.

"Leo!" she whispered.

In a spray of light, he returned. "You sure you don't have something more going on than just a wine order?" he asked teasingly.

Piper socked him on the shoulder. "Are we done with your story?"

"Just about," he answered. "I just thought it was worth passing on because the whole posing as a brother thing sounded so much like the warning about Paige—"

"About some fake sister, somewhere, sometime," Piper interrupted. "The letter didn't mention Paige by name."

"Right. Anyway, it might lend some credence to that story."

"Or it might mean that crazy Agnes became obsessed with the whole idea of fake siblings and went over the deep end," Piper said.

"Maybe," Leo replied. "She must have written

the letter sometime between when she vanquished Timothy and when she died of the
wounds she suffered in battle. The rest of the
family was unaware of it, but they said she died
in the manor."

"Timothy?" Piper asked.

Leo nodded. "That was the warlock's name—
Timothy. Mean anything to you?"

Piper considered it for a moment. "Nope,"
she said. "Now get out of here, and let me finish
with Max. Then we can find Phoebe and try to
straighten this all out."

"Call me." Leo kissed her once and vanished.
Piper quickly finished her count and went to join
Max, intending to do the quickest order of her
career so she and Leo could move on to more
important business.

Paige nearly jumped out of her skin when the
phone rang. She had been sitting in the kitchen,
trying to make sense of what she'd read up in
Phoebe's room. She knew she was late getting
back to work, knew that Mr. Boone's case was still
unresolved, but she couldn't motivate herself to
return to the office. The idea that Phoebe suspected
her of being some kind of phony—or worse, the
possibility that maybe she was a fake and didn't
even know it herself—hung around her neck like a
boulder, dragging her down into despair.

She picked up the phone on the fourth ring.
"Hello," she said listlessly.

"Paige, it's me. Timothy."

The sound of his voice brought a spark of life to her until she remembered that it had been his advice that sent her to Phoebe's room in the first place. "Hi," she said sadly. "I found the letter, Timothy, the one you wanted me to find."

"Doesn't sound like good news," he said. He sounded concerned for her.

"Don't you know what was in it?" she asked him. "You seem to know everything else. You knew it was there. You know this phone number, even though I never gave it to you."

"I'm just trying to help you, Paige. I knew about the letter, that's true. But I thought it was important. If Phoebe doesn't trust you, you need to be aware of that."

"Why?"

"You're the Charmed Ones," he said. "Your lives depend on one another, on being able to know the other sisters are with you at all times. If she's always worried about you, keeping an eye out for you during your battles, then she's going to make a mistake. She'll slip up, and once she's out of the game, both you and Piper are easier targets."

Paige carried the receiver back over to the table and sat down again. "I guess that's true," she said. With her free hand she fiddled with an empty mug someone had left there, spinning it around and around. She felt a little like that, as if she had become trapped on a merry-go-round spinning out of control, and she didn't know how to slow it down or get off. "But how do you know so much about us?"

"I told you, Paige," he said. He sounded so sincere she couldn't bring herself to disbelieve him. Every instinct she had was warning her not to go too far, but some other force, some deep-seated emotion she couldn't put a name to, pushed her toward him. Every time he spoke, it was as if his voice had bypassed all her normal circuits and gone straight to that inner core. The way she trusted him so implicitly was almost unnatural. "You have your powers, I have mine. Maybe I was put here to help you, to protect you, I don't know. Maybe it's just because I like you so much and want to help that I can know these things."

She would have liked to believe that. She would have liked someone to tell her what to believe, since it had all turned so confusing. But first, she would have to know whom to trust. And that was the biggest question, wasn't it? "Maybe, I guess."

"You can't let this defeat you, Paige," Timothy told her. "You need to figure things out, as soon as you can, and put all this behind you."

"You're right, Timothy. But how do I do that?"

"Look around the house," he replied. "Maybe you can find some more of your aunt Agnes's things around. Who knows, a diary, more letters, you know, something that'll at least let you compare handwriting, to make sure that she really wrote that letter or that'll provide some more information. Maybe it'll help you figure out what to do or if she's even a reliable source. If you can convince Phoebe that she was a crazy old nutcase, maybe that'll make everything okay between you."

"I suppose I could look in the attic," Paige said.

"That would be a good place," Timothy answered. "Don't bother with the *Book of Shadows*, though. You know that's the first place Phoebe would have checked."

He was right. Just how often he was right about her sisters was getting downright spooky.

"Okay," she said. "I'll have a look around. Should I call you when I'm done?"

"I'll call you," he said. "Good luck, Paige."

He hung up. Paige looked at the receiver for a long time before she carried it back over to the cradle. *How would he know when to call?* she wondered.

But then, how did he know any of the things he did?

This time, since they all had been together at the meeting, the whole task force converged upon the crime scene at once. Having arrived at the foot of Telegraph Hill in three separate cars, they joined up again and approached the body.

Uniforms had already sealed the scene, a photographer was busy documenting it, and techs waited to one side until it was clear to go in and begin their fine detail work, inspecting every square centimeter for any trace evidence the killer might have left behind.

Once again the victim was female.

"Karen Nakamura," a uniformed officer on the scene announced. "Fifty-three, according to her driver's license. She lives over on Kearny, Telegraph Hill, in one of those condos with a water view."

It meant, Darryl knew, that she was fairly well off. Those condos didn't come cheap. Tugging on disposable latex gloves, he looked at her body, reminding himself that he was a cop and it was his job to put his own feelings aside, to look at her with an impassive eye that would not miss crucial evidence. Stab marks, oddly shaped as before, and damp patches on her designer clothing. The wet killer had struck again.

"Notice what's different?" Monroe Johnson asked him.

Darryl glanced around the crime scene. A quiet street, no apparent witnesses, a woman's corpse. He was about to admit that he didn't when it came to him.

The street was gloomy with fog, but it was still daytime. The other murders had all happened in the dark of night.

"Daylight," he said softly.

Johnson nodded. "Guy's getting bolder. Or more reckless."

"Or both."

"He's picking up the pace, too," Lorraine said from behind them. "Didn't even wait a full twenty-four hours this time, like he has before. The compulsion to kill was too strong to resist. He had to take another victim. Maybe this one let off some of the pressure, or maybe he'll take yet another tonight."

"We have to get this guy off the streets," Stephanie said, joining them.

"That's what I've been saying," Lorraine observed. "What are we still standing around here for?"

"Uniforms are canvassing the neighborhood?" Johnson asked her.

"Yes. They'll let us know if they come up with anything at all. We can't let this body count rise any higher, people. It's already way too high."

Darryl had a brief, unwelcome flash of the house in the Tenderloin, where water in the basement had churned up the remains of almost fifty murder victims. He had barely given that case a moment's consideration since becoming so embroiled in this one. Hundred-year-old skeletons provided precious little in the way of clues, and witnesses to crimes committed a century before were hard to come by. There would be people to whom a solution was important, he knew: descendants of the victims, whose families had never known what had become of their loved ones. Funerals with empty coffins, memorialized in photos that begat difficult questions but provided no answers.

But he knew whoever had killed those fifty was no longer a threat. He needed to find this so-called wet killer before his modern-day body count reached the same horrible number.

"Scobie, Payzant," Lorraine was saying, "you two work this one, Nakamura. Get to know her. Find out where she was coming from, where she was going. Does she have a family? A husband? A lover? Get to them. Check her job, her car, her pets. Anything and everything."

"Got it, boss," Leonard Scobie said.

"The rest of you, you have jobs to do and you know what they are," Lorraine said. "I want a line on this guy by the time the sun goes down. He's going to kill again, and I want to be there to stop him before he does."

Chapter
9

Cole had gone for a walk around the Tenderloin District that morning, checking out the building that Piper and Leo had told him about. It wasn't hard to find: Yellow police tape still sealed off the door and windows from prying eyes, and the building next door was still fronted by scaffolding from the renovation job that had loosed the water into the basement to begin with. There was a sour, mildewy odor emanating from the apartment building that Cole figured must have been from standing water, maybe mixed with the smell of old bones and long-ago death.

Once he'd found it and gotten as good a look as he could from the outside, he noted the address and headed for City Hall, just a short hike away. The Tenderloin was one of San Francisco's poorest neighborhoods, full of the downtrodden, down-at-their-heels, or just plain down-and-out. Some mornings, this one included, it seemed that there were more people living on its streets than under its roofs. Just a few blocks away some of San Francisco's most spectacular old buildings rose up, looking as if they'd been imported from the capitals of Europe. Cole walked between the massive structures, surrounded by fences topped with spear tips of gold, until he reached the domed French Renaissance masterpiece that was City Hall itself. Cole Turner had spent plenty of time here in his assistant district attorney days, and he kept his head down, looking at the marble floor as he entered instead of up at the magnificent staircase and rotunda, hoping that he wouldn't be recognized.

Having made it safely to the city's records department, he relaxed a little. There was plenty of turnover here, and the chance that anyone behind the counter would recognize him from those days was slim to none. After he'd waited a few moments, a pretty Asian girl came out from a back room and tossed him a cheery smile. She wore a tight red silk shirt and tighter black stretch pants with heels that couldn't have been comfortable but added a few inches to her height. "I'll be right with you," she said brightly. He caught a whiff of a musky, exotic perfume he didn't recognize. It wouldn't have worked on Piper, but it was lovely on this young woman.

He smiled back. "Take your time."

She crossed to her desk, picked up the phone, and punched the button for a line. After a brief conversation, during which she reported the results of something she had looked up for the caller, she hung up again. "Sorry about that," she said. "Is there something I can help you with?"

He wrote the address down on a slip of paper. "I need ownership records for this building," he said.

She glanced at it. "Not a problem. Current owners?"

"No," Cole told her. "Let's say from 1880 to 1910."

She lowered the paper and gave him a curious look. "O-kay," she said. "You're, um, not in a hurry, are you?"

"I have some time," he said. He looked around the waiting area, but there were no chairs. "I'll just make myself comfortable here. Standing."

"You do that," she said. She took the slip of paper and went back into the file room.

Twenty-two minutes later she returned with a thin, ancient-looking file folder in her hands. "Still here," she said. "Most people give up if it takes longer than five minutes."

"The short attention span society," Cole replied. "Too much *Sesame Street* and MTV."

She laughed. "That's it exactly." She set the folder down on the counter and opened it.

"Anyway, the property you're interested in seems to have quite the history. Built by a man named Herman Gates, who died intestate. The city ended up taking possession when poor Mr. Gates proved to have no heirs and also, conveniently, proved to owe large sums in municipal fees and back taxes. There was a brief battle with the state, which also wanted the property, but the city won."

She leaned against the counter and ran her fingers back and forth across the outside of the file. Cole was starting to think she had more on her mind than just helping a citizen look up a record. There had been a time in his life when he might have been interested, but he was with Phoebe now, and anyone else paled in comparison.

"He had already leased out some of the building as apartments, so the city simply divided up the part he was living in as more of the same," she said, her voice a little huskier than it had been a moment ago. "Hired a manager to . . . well, manage the place, I guess. So, while I don't know exactly what you're looking for, I thought, maybe what he needs isn't just ownership records, but tenant records. Because the city owned it for most of the period you're talking about, but a variety of different people rented there. If the city hadn't owned it, you'd be out of luck because we wouldn't have tenant listings." She caught his gaze and held it. "But we do, so it looks like your lucky day."

Cole swallowed. "I'm, um, interested in a basement apartment."

"Basement apartments are rare in San Francisco," she said. Her breath smelled like wintergreen. "My place is on the fourth floor. If you lean way out the window and look to the right, you can see Alcatraz."

"Cheerful view," he replied nervously. "Do you know who had the basement apartment during that period?"

The young woman sighed and flipped open the file folder. "Flora Jackson, to 1901. Then Hans Schieffel for a few months. He died. After 1901 . . . oh, this is interesting."

"What?"

"The last tenant down there was someone named Timothy McBride. According to a note here, he simply disappeared in 1904. He had paid his rent in advance, so he wasn't skipping out on that. Just went out one day and never came back. After that, other tenants began moving out, and the city had a hard time renting the apartments at all. They put the building up for sale in 1911, just to cut their losses."

"So there was never anyone living in the basement after this McBride?"

"That's what it shows. Until a William Levine bought the property in 1912, but that's after when you said you were interested in."

"That's right," Cole said. "You've been very helpful, thank you."

She fluttered her eyelashes at him, a trick he'd thought had gone out with forties movies. It worked for her, though. "You could come by my place later on," she told him. "You wouldn't have to look at Alcatraz, but I could show you heaven on earth."

"That's a very generous offer," Cole replied. "But I, uh, left my heart in San Francisco."

She scowled. "If you knew how many times a day I hear that."

Cole retreated quickly, again keeping his gaze on the floor until he was safely outside. For as uncomfortable as it had become, that hadn't been as helpful as he'd hoped, although he wasn't sure exactly what he might be able to learn from the old records. He had a name at least. Timothy McBride, no forwarding address, was a likely suspect just because of the way he had vanished without notice. The fact that no one wanted to rent there after him meant something too. Cole knew enough about the world not to discount what many so-called rational people would have: that the scene of so many murders would have left an unpleasant vibration, at the very least, in the apartment. Almost no one would have been comfortable there, with the possible exception of the killer, who might have felt right at home.

But he still had no way to track this McBride character, no clue to where he might have gone after leaving the slaughterhouse behind. He didn't know what good it would do, but he'd get together with Piper and Leo, after he met Phoebe to see how her interview went, and maybe by then they could supply more pieces of the puzzle.

Following Timothy's advice, though, the way things had been turning out so far, she wasn't entirely sure why, Paige went up to the attic to see if she could find any more traces of Aunt Agnes. Climbing the stairs, she felt as if her legs were weighted with concrete blocks. There seemed to be every reason in the world to drop this whole thing right now and no reason to go on.

Well, there was one reason. She wanted to prove that she was a Charmed One, loyal to the family and their mission. If this whole thing had come up right away, when she'd first met Piper and Phoebe, she might have welcomed the chance to dodge what seemed to be her fate. But now she was committed. She was in it for keeps, she knew, whether they accepted it or not.

When she had been in the fifth grade, before her own rebellious nature had put her on the outs with her parents, there had been a time that they all had gone together as a family to a mall. But her dad had an agenda of his own, and her mom had wanted to look at some stores that Paige would have found deathly boring, so they had agreed that she could take off by herself, as

long as she met them at the mall entrance at a
certain time. At first the freedom had felt liberat-
ing, but after a while she had begun to feel
lonely. Then she had gone to the place where she
believed they had agreed to meet, but no parents
had been there. She had waited and waited with
a growing sense of unease. Strangers passing by
began to look less interesting and more sinister.
Paige had been starting to wonder if she'd been
abandoned by her parents when finally her dad
had come along, frantic, and she learned that she
had completely misunderstood which entrance
they were supposed to meet, and her parents,
worried sick about her, had been at the other one
for thirty minutes.

Now she was getting the same feeling about
her sisters, the sense that they were abandoning
her, somehow, by not trusting her or being willing to talk about it.

When she opened the attic door, Paige was
struck by another wave of helplessness. The attic
was the repository of just about everything the
descendants of Melinda Warren had left behind.
There were boxes, filing cabinets, desks, dressers,
more boxes, steamer trunks, suitcases, and then
still more boxes. Since nothing seemed to have
neon arrows pointing to it or "AGNES" written
in big letters on the side, she didn't have a clue
where to begin looking. Every minute she spent
here in some fruitless search was one more
minute that Mr. Cowan would be flipping out

wondering where she was. She should have called, she knew, an hour ago.

But at least there was something she could do about that. She held out one hand and said, "Phone." The handset orbed into her hand, and she dialed Cowan's direct line. When he came on, she said, "Mr. Cowan, this is Paige Matthews."

"I've heard that name before," he growled. "That's right, there was a Paige Matthews who *used* to work here. But she—"

"Mr. Cowan, I'm sorry I didn't call sooner," she interrupted him. "I came home for lunch and suddenly started feeling woozy. I lay down for a minute and just now woke up. I have a fever, and . . . well, I guess I'm sick."

"You don't sound good," he said. That worried her a little since she hadn't been intentionally trying to sound ill. Maybe it was just the depression she felt over the Aunt Agnes letter showing itself in her voice.

"Yeah, that's because I'm not," she said. "I'm very not good. I'm sure I'll be okay tomorrow, though, if I can just get some more sleep."

"Be here on time, Matthews," he said. She could picture him tugging on his goatee as he spoke, a habit he had when he was particularly angry or on edge. It sometimes made her wonder how he had any facial hair left at all. "Or don't show up at all." He hung up.

That went well, she thought sarcastically.

Typical anyway. She orbed the phone back to where it belonged and tackled the nearest box.

After a few cartons she had developed a system. She would crack open a box, and at a glance she could tell the approximate age of most of its contents. There was a remarkable variety of interesting-looking items in the boxes, making her want to spend more time with them. It was a little like Christmas in an antiques store, with the extra advantage that none of the things in the boxes had a price tag. But today she had a specific goal in mind. Gradually it dawned on her that cardboard boxes were more of a mid- to late-twentieth-century thing, and that what she was after predated that by a wide margin. She turned her attention to older storage devices.

Finally, she found what she was looking for: an old trunk, its hasp rusty but unlocked, its sides black with age and wear. She pushed the lid back, and written in a fine, scratchy pen on the inside was the name AGNES HALLIWELL. The handwriting looked remarkably like that which she'd seen on the letter in Phoebe's room, and Paige's heart sank.

Inside the trunk she found a white lace shawl that was still in remarkably good shape and beneath that, wrapped in tissue-like paper that was so old it crumbled in her fingertips, a couple of soft silk blouses, both cream-colored. There was a separate wooden box inside the trunk, which Paige took to be a jewelry box until she

opened it. It wasn't. Inside, she found an
athame, several candles, a couple of stoppered
glass jars containing the dusty remains of what
had once been herbs, a wooden mortar and pestle,
and, wrapped in their own felt bundle, several
small crystals. Aunt Agnes's collection of magical implements. In spite of the trouble the
woman had caused, Paige felt a deep connection
to Agnes at this moment. She carefully closed
the box and dug through the rest of the items in
the trunk, mostly clothing that had seen better
days. But tucked between two worn sweaters
was one more interesting object, an old hand
mirror with a beautifully worked cameo back
showing a pastoral scene and golden scallops
framing the glass. Paige couldn't resist looking
at herself in the glass, which was bright and
clear in spite of the mirror's obvious age.

As she did, she heard the distant sound of the
telephone. Remembering that she was supposed
to be home sick, she orbed it back again.

"This is Paige," she said, trying this time to
sound bedraggled.

"Paige, it's Timothy. Everything okay?"

"How do you do that?" she wondered. "I just
this very moment finished going through Aunt
Agnes's trunk."

"What did you find? Anything helpful?" he
asked.

"No, not really. Her old magical tools, some
clothing, a really lovely mirror. That's about it."

Timothy was quiet for a moment. When he spoke again, his voice carried a new tone, one she hadn't heard before. He sounded uneasy, maybe worried. "Paige, I don't want to have to tell you this, but I think you might be in some danger there."

She laughed but then realized how sincere he had sounded. "I'm sorry, Timothy. But in danger here? This is, like, the safest place in the world for me."

"You're wrong. If you could trust your sisters, if they trusted you, then sure, it would be. But until you can convince them that you really are their sister, and not some impostor or fraud, that's not a good place for you to be. In a demonic attack or something, they wouldn't have any idea where you'd stand. They'd be dodging you as well as the demons. Someone could get seriously hurt, and I'm afraid it might be you."

What he left unsaid, of course, was that Phoebe and Piper might just turn against her if they were convinced of the truth contained in Aunt Agnes's letter. Paige didn't believe a word of it, but she had to admit that finding the same handwriting on the trunk's lid added some weight to the letter's authenticity.

"What do you think I should do?" she asked him.

"Let's get together and talk in person," Timothy said. "We can figure something out. I know we can. And I can help protect you until we do."

Paige thought it over for about ten seconds. It wouldn't be bad to see Timothy again. He really had been on her side through this whole ordeal, she knew. And he sounded so reassuring she could even allow herself to believe that she would get past it all. With his help.

"Where are you?" she asked.

"Meet me in Golden Gate Park," he said. "By the Dutch windmill. Half an hour."

"Okay," she said. "I'll see you there."

"Oh, Paige," he said, stopping her before she could hang up, "bring Aunt Agnes's mirror, too."

"The mirror?" Paige echoed. "Why?"

"Just something I want to try with it," Timothy told her. "I think it'll help."

Paige shrugged. "Okay," she said again. "Whatever. See you there."

She hung up the phone and orbed it back downstairs, then picked up the lovely mirror again. She felt better than she had since she'd found the letter. At least she was doing something, taking steps toward figuring this whole crazy situation out.

And she knew she'd have Timothy by her side the whole way.

Well, that couldn't have gone much worse, Phoebe thought as she left her interview. Michael Langdon, after questioning her awhile longer, had taken her back into the warehouse to show her the facility. But it had been so dusty back there that she'd started sneezing uncontrollably. Finally, Langdon had taken her back into his office and given her a box of tissues and a cup of water, then had gone into a cupboard for a can of Lysol and started spraying every object Phoebe might have touched. "Can't afford to get sick, you know," he told her.

"I'm not sick," she told him, sniffling. "It's just all the dust."

"Still, it's best not to take chances."

After her sneezing had come under control and he'd emptied half a can of antibacterial spray, he promised to call her within a week and had shown her the door. Somehow, as she stepped through it, she was pretty sure she'd never see the inside of that place again. And just as certain that she didn't want to.

Before she even reached the Jeep, Leo and Piper orbed into sight in front of her.

"Well, hello," Phoebe said. "Come to see where I won't be working?"

"We have some news," Piper said. "We don't think it's the good kind of news."

"About what?" Phoebe asked her.

"About Aunt Agnes. For starters." Piper glanced at the traffic rushing past them, both pedestrian and automotive. "Can we go someplace a little more private and talk?"

"I was supposed to meet Cole at City Brew,"

Phoebe said. "He was going to buy me a celebratory latte. Or a consolatory one. Looks like it'll be the latter latte." She paused. "Try saying *that* ten times fast."

"Is he there now?" Leo asked.

"He should be."

"Leave the car," he said. "I'll drive."

A mini light show later, they all were standing outside City Brew. Cole saw them arrive and instantly swept Phoebe into his arms.

"How'd it go?" he asked, kissing her gently on the lips. She liked the kiss a lot more than the answer she had to give.

"Not well. I'll give you all the gory details later, though. Apparently there are more pressing matters afoot, and there's something else we have to take care of this afternoon." She hadn't forgotten the woman in her vision, whom they still needed to find before nightfall. And nightfall was getting closer all the time.

City Brew was a neighborhood coffee shop that did a brisk morning business but was relatively quiet the rest of the day. Its decor was strictly thrift shop chic, mismatched tables and chairs and a few low sofas, with a counter that had been refashioned from the bar of the saloon that had occupied this space from sometime in the forties. They went inside, ordered their drinks, and sat down on a collection of comfy chairs far from the nearest other patrons.

"Here's what I found out, in a nutshell," Leo

said once they were settled. "Agnes fought with the family because she was protecting a warlock named Timothy, who had been murdering innocents and had fooled her into thinking he was really her brother. Once she realized he'd been playing her, she took him on and vanquished him. But in the battle he wounded her, a wound that turned out to be fatal. End of Agnes, end of story."

"Except not," Cole said.

"Why not?" Phoebe asked. Her latte was still too hot to drink, so she blew on it as she listened.

"Because unless there's a remarkable coincidence here, Timothy pops up yet again."

"The Tenderloin house?" Leo asked.

Cole nodded. "One Timothy McBride rented the basement apartment there. He disappeared without a trace, even though he was ahead on the rent. After he vanished, nobody else wanted to rent the place; nobody wanted to rent anywhere in the building, for that matter. The city had to unload the place."

"And that's body central," Piper said. She licked foam from her upper lip.

"Correct," Cole said. "I'm guessing all those corpses were why old Timothy didn't get his cleaning deposit back."

"Well, that and the fact that Aunt Agnes had vanquished him," Phoebe added, "which makes it hard to get your mail."

"So let me see if I have this straight," Phoebe

said. "Agnes was involved in something that sounds a lot like the letter we have, supposedly from her, only in her case, she's the one who fell for the phony sibling routine. The phony sibling in question was this Timothy whatever—"

"McBride," Cole put in.

"—and she vanquished him, but he killed her too. Meanwhile he was busy killing fifty or so people and putting them in his basement."

"Which is why the family was after him," Piper said. "Because even then Halliwells protected the innocent, and he was killing innocents."

Phoebe shot her a you're-interrupting look but didn't say anything. "And now, coincidentally, we get a letter warning us about a very similar occurrence, that we think—"

"*You* think," Piper interrupted again.

"—some of us think might possibly be in reference to Paige. At the same time, the bodies of this Timothy's victims turn up. Also at the same time, there's a killer roaming around San Francisco, murdering women."

"That part still could be a coincidence," Leo commented, "but I don't think so."

"I don't either," Cole said. "I think it sounds like Agnes's old friend Timothy has come back to visit."

"Can that happen?" Phoebe asked. "If he was vanquished?"

"It would depend on how she did it, what

kind of spell she used," Leo answered. "The short answer is yes, under certain circumstances. Especially if she was badly wounded and losing power."

Piper tentatively raised a hand as if she were back in school. "Does anyone else think we should maybe find Paige?"

Cole fished a cell phone out of his jacket pocket and handed it to Piper. She dialed Paige's office, spoke for a minute to whoever answered, and then disconnected. "Paige is home sick," she announced, looking at Leo.

"I know," Leo said. He glanced around to make sure no one was watching and orbed them all back to the manor. Phoebe still hadn't touched her latte.

But the manor, they found, was empty. Phoebe thought that someone might have been in her room while she was away, but she wasn't certain. The drawer in her nightstand could have been canted at a slightly different angle from the way she usually left it, and there was a trace odor that might have been Paige's perfume, but it was too faint to know for sure. They went floor to floor, and after a few moments Piper called to them from the attic, panicked urgency in her voice. Phoebe took the stairs three at a time.

When they got there, Piper, her face etched with concern, showed them an old worn trunk standing open in the middle of the floor. Phoebe didn't remember having seen it before. "That's what has you so upset?" she asked. "Luggage?"

"I found it open like this," she said. "I'm pretty sure Paige has been here." She pointed to a scrawl on the inside of its lid: the name Agnes Halliwell.

"Oh, crap!" Phoebe exclaimed.

"My sentiments exactly," Piper said.

Chapter 10

"I think we need some expert assistance here," Leo said. With no further explanation, he orbed out of the attic, leaving the two Halliwell sisters and Cole staring at one another, dumbfounded.

"Where's he going?" Phoebe demanded.

Piper shrugged. "I'm his wife, not his keeper."

"It does seem like a strange time to up and vanish," Cole observed.

"I don't know if you've realized it, Cole," Piper said, still on her knees by the trunk, "but to most of the world, vanishing at all would be considered pretty strange. We have a different standard for strange."

"Well, I don't think we should waste time worrying about him," Phoebe said. "We have plenty to do here. We need to figure out what is, or was, in this trunk that Paige found and see if there's a clue to where she might have gone. And how it all ties together with this Timothy McBride and the murders. Also, we have to do it soon because there's going to be another murder tonight if we don't stop it."

Piper turned away from examining the trunk, which wasn't really getting her anywhere, and fixed Phoebe with a steady gaze. "Vision?"

Phoebe nodded.

"And you were going to tell us about it when?"

Phoebe shrugged. "I'm, um, telling you now?"

"You actually had a premonition of this McBride killing someone?" Cole asked.

"Well, I don't know for sure if it was McBride since I don't know what he looks like. And I really didn't get a good look at the killer anyway. The whole scene was dark and foggy. I would recognize the woman, though. Kind of pretty, olive skin, dark hair, wearing a uniform. Like a waitress's uniform."

"But you haven't had visions of any of the earlier killings," Piper said, "even though we think they're all the work of this same warlock."

"That's right."

"So," Cole said, "maybe that means he's becoming more powerful, a greater threat? And therefore he's showing up on your radar when he didn't before?"

"Possible, I suppose," Piper said. "Did you

recognize the uniform, Phoebe? Or the location? Anything to help us stop it?"

"Not really," Phoebe said glumly. "Stains on her shoes that could have been clam chowder. I got a distinct seafoody sensation from her."

Piper raised her hands in dismay, thinking of all the seafood places she'd eaten in, not to mention the many more that she hadn't. "That narrows it down to maybe only a thousand places spread all over the city."

"I didn't say it was a helpful premonition," Phoebe replied. "I just said I had one."

"We'll just have to work on finding McBride before he strikes again," Cole said.

Piper took a deep breath, forcing herself to broach a subject that had been on her mind for a while now. "There's something else I think we should work on," she said, fixing Phoebe with a steady gaze.

"What?"

"You and I. We've been at each other's throats ever since you had that dream."

Phoebe nodded. "Because you didn't want to give the letter any credence, and I did."

"Right," Piper said. "But it doesn't strike you as just a little bit odd how immediately and thoroughly we disagreed? It's like we can't even talk about it."

"So what are we doing now?" Phoebe asked with an edge of bitterness in her voice.

"That's what I mean," Piper continued. "It's

taking every ounce of self-restraint I can muster not to start yelling at you or something. And I'm betting you feel the same way."

"Maybe . . ."

"And it's not just about Paige, is it?"

Phoebe considered this for a moment. "I guess not," she said. "It's more . . . I don't know. General."

"Exactly," Piper said firmly. "Do you think we've been enchanted somehow? That we're at odds because we've been magically ordered to be?"

"It makes sense, Phoebe," Cole interjected. "More sense than the idea that Piper has just suddenly become a stubborn old—" He cut himself off in mid-sentence. "Not that you would say anything like that."

Phoebe didn't answer but instead started flipping rapidly through the pages of the *Book of Shadows*. Piper thought she was deliberately ignoring the situation, and that annoyed her. *But then again*, she realized, *maybe it's the spell that's annoying me. I just wish I could know my own mind.* "What are you doing?" she asked finally.

Phoebe stopped paging through the book long enough to give her an exasperated frown. "Looking for a counterspell."

There was a sudden shimmering in the air, and Leo reappeared. He wasn't alone. The woman with him was old but projected an air of strength. Her shoulders were broad, her back was straight, and she held her silvered head at an imperious angle. She had small, very pale blue eyes, and she looked down at the Halliwell sisters as if from a great height, even though she was only an inch or so taller than they were. Piper knew at once that she was a ghost and even had a guess about whose.

"Maybe we can help with that," Leo said, referring, Piper supposed, to Cole's last comment. "Piper, Phoebe, meet your aunt Agnes."

Piper had already figured that out, but from the shocked expression on Phoebe's face, she guessed that her sister had not. "But I thought—"

"You thought I wanted nothing to do with the Halliwell family," Agnes said. Her voice was cold and hard, like a dagger of ice.

"Well, basically, yes."

"You were right," Agnes told them. "I didn't. I don't. But your Leo—" Her gaze sought out Piper, held on her. "Your Leo, I believe?"

Piper wasn't quite sure how to answer that. "I—I guess so, yes."

"Your Leo," she went on, not even waiting for Piper's response, "convinced me that Timothy McBride has somehow returned."

"That's the way we understand it," Piper said.

"I vanquished him once, you know."

"That's what we heard," Phoebe said. "Which is why we're not quite sure how or why he's back."

"I'm not at all certain about that myself," Agnes said. "Tell me, Piper, since you seem to be pawing through my things, is there a hand mirror in that trunk?"

Piper hadn't seen one, but then she hadn't been looking for it, either. She checked again. "I'm not seeing one."

Agnes let out a long sigh. "I was afraid of that," she said ominously.

"Why don't you tell us what happened?" Leo asked. "And what this mirror has to do with anything. These young ladies have another sister out there somewhere, and we're afraid she may have become mixed up in this."

"Very well," Agnes replied. "Now, this all happened a hundred years ago, you understand."

Phoebe leaned against an old rolltop desk, evidently expecting a long story. Piper crossed her legs, making herself more comfortable as well.

Agnes remained ramrod straight. She wore a white blouse with vertical pleats, tucked at her narrow waist into a long, plain black skirt. Her hands rested at her sides. "I didn't say it was boring, ladies, I just said it happened a long time ago. Things needn't be brand-new to be exciting. We had plenty of excitement in my day, I can assure all of you."

"Agnes . . . ," Leo said, prodding her gently.

"Very well. I can see that patience is one more

excellent character trait long since out of fashion."

"We're just concerned about our sister," Phoebe said. "And another woman I saw in a premonition. She's in danger too."

Agnes gave a harrumph. "All right," she said. "I'll skip over the unnecessary parts and get right to the gist of it. I met a warlock named Timothy McBride. He was quite pleasant, handsome, and polite, and he told me that he was a witch. As we talked, it became clear that we had much in common. We talked longer, and I realized that it was more than that: It seemed that he was my long-lost half brother, a son my mother had borne after she had lost contact with the rest of the family."

"Like Paige," Phoebe interjected.

Agnes ignored her and went on. "Timothy and I had several long conversations, and we both came to accept sincerely that we were siblings. Or at least that's what I thought. But during this same period there was a warlock taking innocents from all over the city. People were terrified. They didn't know where their friends and loved ones were going. We believed they were being killed by a warlock, who had somehow figured out a way to obtain power through the deaths of regular people, not just witches. So we all were trying to find the warlock, and then the rest of the family decided that it was Timothy."

She sniffed once, angrily, as if just now remembering the indignity of it all. "Well, I just couldn't let myself believe that about my newly found brother. He was the nicest man I'd ever met and certainly no killer. So when they accused him, I rushed to his defense. I told them that they were wrong; they could not possibly have the right witch. Then I went to Timothy and warned him. I told him he would have to watch himself, and that if he could help me prove his innocence, I would stand by him.

"As it turned out," she continued, "I did more than that. I hid him from the rest of the family. I fought off my own sisters' spells. I sheltered him. The family has always hated me because of that; they still hate me, to this day. And I haven't forgiven them for that, for the way they treated me.

"Even though they were right and I was wrong."

Something like real sorrow shone in her eyes then, and Piper was surprised, as always, to remember that emotions didn't die with a person's physical body. Aches and pains went away, but those things that really hurt—and, she supposed, the ones that brought genuine happiness—stayed as long as consciousness did. Death, she had learned, was not an ending at all but merely a transition, and a person was essentially the same on the other side of it.

"I didn't realize it until one day when I was with Timothy at the place where we'd been hiding out, in an apartment he had rented in the

Tenderloin. I was trying to locate a sister, scrying with the help of an enchanted mirror I owned, when Timothy happened to pass behind the mirror. And in the reflection I saw not the handsome, strong brother I thought I had, but a twisted, evil being, the monster he really was. He had fooled my senses with some sort of glamour, but he could not trick the mirror."

That must be the mirror that she had me look for, Piper thought. *The mirror that should be in the trunk but isn't. And, since we're thinking Paige opened the trunk, maybe the mirror she has with her now.*

Agnes went on with her tale, her tone less one of sorrow than of pent-up anger at this point. "I knew then that he had fooled me, used me to protect him against the rest of the family. I was furious, but when I tried to face him, to confront him about it, all I could see was the Timothy I had trusted. I still couldn't bring myself to do battle with him: He was evil, I had come to accept that, but he was still family. And he, realizing that I knew something, was preparing himself to kill me. I had to take action, and I had to do it immediately. So I looked at his reflection in the mirror again, and using that as a tool, I cast my vanquishing spell at his true face, his reflection."

"And you successfully vanquished him," Leo said.

"I thought I had," Agnes said, "although in

the battle he also wounded me, fatally as it turned out. I cast his physical being into the mirror, where he would be held, I expected, forever. But from what you've told me, perhaps I was wrong. Maybe some aspect of his essence remained outside the mirror, and he is working on returning to his full physical form, again amassing power by killing innocents."

"That's what it sounds like," Leo said.

"So do you know how we can find him? Stop him?" Phoebe asked.

"I'm not altogether sure," Agnes replied. "Since I apparently didn't do as good a job as I believed in the first place. But one thing's for certain."

"What's that?" Piper inquired.

"You need to find that mirror," the ghost insisted, "before he does."

Darryl Morris sat at his desk in the open bullpen, gazing between half-open miniblinds at the foggy street beyond his window. The police station was a riot of noise and activity. The day's weather had been the cause of dozens of traffic accidents, large and small. In one case a taxi had misjudged the speed of an oncoming cable car and tried to make a left turn in front of it. The cable car's enormous steel bumper had caught the cab's left-front fender and ripped a huge gash in it, but to make matters worse, it had pushed the cab back into a traffic light control box, taking out the light.

Traffic had snarled behind that accident and many of the others, resulting in arguments, fights, and in one case a shooting incident, though fortunately the shooter had missed his target, and the bullet, while shattering the window of an Italian tailor shop, hadn't hurt anyone. San Francisco had remarkably consistent weather, Darryl knew, with a temperature variation from winter to summer of less than twenty degrees. But as consistent as it was, the city could really be impacted by an anomaly like extra-thick pea soup.

Since viewing the Nakamura crime scene, he had been back at his desk, pulling the phone records of all the victims and comparing them. His eyes were sore from staring at the rows of numbers, and a throbbing headache was building behind his temples. But that didn't matter; he would push himself and drive as hard as he had to in order to bring this killer in.

He learned that both Julia Tilton and Rosa Porfiro had called the same movie theater's recorded ticket information line in the past ten days, but not on the same day, so the chance that they'd been at the movie together was slim. Wells, Nakamura, and Winter all had called 555-1212 for the correct time in the past thirty days, but that was meaningless. So had Darryl himself, and that call was strictly automated. And four days ago Nakamura had called a number that Tilton had called nineteen days before that,

a number that turned out, when Darryl tried it,
to be the complaint line for missed newspaper
deliveries.

As far as he could tell, the rest of the task
force was turning up equally empty-handed, in
terms of connecting the victims to one another. It
left only one possibility: The murders were random, crimes of opportunity. And the killer would
be that much harder to find.

Paige had always loved Golden Gate Park, even
as a little girl. She didn't spend nearly as much
time there as she would have liked, but just
knowing it was there, a green respite from the
miles of concrete and steel that made up the rest
of the city, brought her a certain peace of mind
when she thought of it. She enjoyed the muse-
ums, the enforced stillness of the Japanese tea
garden, the stunning array of flora in the conser-
vatory, watching the boats on Stow Lake or the
miniature ones on Spreckels Lake, or just walking the many paths and meadows. The variety of
trees on these few miles was mind-boggling,
from spreading oaks to imported eucalyptus,
with its constantly peeling bark, to enormous
redwoods reaching for the clouds.

In junior high, she had done a report on the
Dutch windmill, and she remembered some of
what her research had shown. The land from
which the park had been sculpted had originally
been sand dunes, with no water except from the

nearby ocean. To make from these sandy wastes a park containing a million trees, vast grassy tracts, and abundant flora of every description, not to mention nine lakes, required the movement of huge amounts of water. To that end in 1903 the city erected the Dutch windmill at the park's northwest corner, looking and functioning just like its cousins in the Netherlands. The massive concrete structure, seventy-five feet tall with arms more than a hundred feet long, was able to pump thirty thousand gallons of water an hour, water that, naturally filtered through the sand dunes, was pure enough to fill and maintain the freshwater lakes. A second windmill, at the southwest corner, was erected shortly after, but both were eventually replaced by electric pumps. Now the structures remained as curiosities but had no practical value beyond that.

Today the fog had come in thick off the ocean, making Paige glad she'd worn her leather jacket, and she could barely see the domed top of the windmill. The upper sections of the spars were completely hidden from view. Fog drifted through the surrounding trees like smoke from a forest fire, obscuring their upper leaves and branches and even the trunks of those not immediately adjacent to the clearing around the windmill's base. The tulips and daffodils planted around the windmill were not in bloom, but in the soft gray light the pink and white and magenta rhododendrons were almost shockingly vibrant.

She couldn't see Timothy anywhere, though. She stood in the center of the grassy sward by the windmill, next to the flower beds there, and turned in a slow circle. The day was so cold and dismal that there were no tourists about and none of the weddings that were often held here in the structure's shadow. For a moment she thought she saw someone looking down at her from the wooden decking that surrounded the windmill about a third of the way up, but then the fog shifted, and she realized she'd been wrong; it had been a trick of the light. The only sounds she heard were the distant rumble of surf from across the Great Highway and the occasional creaking of the skeletal wooden spars as the wind blew through them. When the windmill was functional, the spars had been covered with canvas sails, and the breeze didn't pass through uselessly but turned the arms, working the pump mechanism behind the building's five-foot-thick walls.

All in all, she thought, *this is a surprisingly spooky place when there's no one else around.* "Timothy?" she called, hoping he was here somewhere, maybe just hidden by the roiling clouds of fog. "Where are you?"

A full minute passed, maybe more, before he answered. "Back here, Paige," he said, sounding strangely distant. "In the trees."

She looked toward where she thought the sound of his voice had come from, a thick growth of trees across the grassy patch and flower beds from the windmill. The trunks were whitish, almost invisible in the fog, their leaves high off the ground. Staring through the mist between the trees, she finally spotted a pale oval that she thought must be Timothy's face.

"What are you doing in there?" she asked with a nervous chuckle. "Come on out here."

"It's safer in the trees," Timothy replied. "You come on in here."

"Safer?" she echoed. "Safe from what?" But she started toward him anyway.

He didn't answer Paige's question, asking his own instead. "Did you bring the mirror?"

Even as she approached the tree line, Timothy's face didn't seem to resolve itself into anything more substantial but remained floating, almost ghostlike, in the fog. She wasn't sure what was going on—why he was being so mysterious and cautious or especially why he was so concerned with Aunt Agnes's looking glass— and she found the whole situation more than a little troubling. Everything he had done for her, everything he said just raised more questions than answers. As she threaded her way among the spectral tree trunks, Paige decided she wanted some answers, and she wanted them now. She didn't want to think of herself as the kind of girl who would take a virtual stranger's word over that of her sisters, and he had pushed her just about as far as she was willing to go.

"What are you doing, Timothy?" she asked again. "Come on, I'm not going to bite you."

"Answer me," Timothy replied, his voice suddenly more firm and commanding than he had been in the past and maybe a little bit angry. The change unnerved her. "Did you bring it?"

"You told me to," she replied flatly. "Of course I brought it. But I'd like you to answer some questions too."

"I will, I promise, Paige." Now he sounded more like the Timothy she had come to know, however superficially. "But I just need the mirror. Give it to me, and I'll answer everything you want. Anything."

"Well, come and get it then." She didn't want to do all the walking through the underbrush, thicker now away from the windmill's open area, but wanted him at least to meet her halfway. Especially since he was showing signs of not being exactly the nice guy she had believed him to be. She took the mirror from her backpack purse and showed it to him. As the fog drifted between them, he seemed to waver and disappear, then become more distinct when the fog passed. She still thought it was just the fading daylight and the thick mist playing tricks on her, but she was less sure with every moment.

"Put the mirror down, there in that open spot," he said, pointing. She saw where he meant, a tiny clearing among four trees where no underbrush grew and the ground was matted with fallen leaves. "Then back away, and I'll come and get it."

"What's the matter with you, Timothy?" Paige wanted to know. "Why won't you just take it from my hand?" She remembered now that she had never once touched him, that even when she'd given him her phone number, he had waited until she put it down on the table before he had taken it. Suddenly that fact seemed very significant to her, although she wasn't quite sure what it might mean. "Is something wrong with you? Are you sick or something?"

"Paige," Timothy said abruptly, "just put the mirror down and walk away."

She waved it toward him teasingly. "What's the big deal? I want to know, Timothy. I want you to tell me."

"I already told you that I'd answer all your questions, Paige. Just please do as I ask. Put the mirror down there. I'll come and get it, and everything will be fine. I can't explain, can't tell you why I don't want to get too close to you yet. But after you give me the mirror, everything will be okay. We'll be able to be together, Paige. For as long as we want, you and I."

She couldn't deny that she had been thinking along the same lines, at least until this new, creepier Timothy had shown himself. He had appeared to be everything she wanted: hand-some, nice, fun to be with, and comfortable with her witchiness in a way that none of the other men she knew would ever be. Of course she didn't know him well enough to know if there really were grounds for a serious relationship. It was surprising to hear him talking as if a romance between them were simply assumed, surprising yet, in a strange way, exciting and complimen-tary. She liked the take-charge kind of guy, and the fact that this one obviously thought she was attractive was very appealing.

So the bit with the mirror was a little weird. Nothing wrong with that, was there? After all, she was a witch, and a few months ago she'd have thought that was way out there on the bizarre scale too. She wasn't really one, she decided, to judge others on the basis of their weirdness quotients.

Anyway, she was a powerful witch now. No matter what his deal was, she was sure he didn't mean her any harm. And if for some reason he did, she'd just cope. She had defended her life many times and could do it again against any threat that might arise now.

But the fact was, she really couldn't bring her-self to doubt him, even though she thought maybe she should. It was as if there were a gov-ernor on her credibility-judging mechanism, keeping her from questioning too much. Every time she began to distrust him her emotions grew agitated, and when she gave herself over to belief, everything calmed down. She had always considered herself a good judge of character, and something inside her told her that Timothy, despite obvious weirdnesses, was a good guy.

"Okay," she said at last. "But I'm telling you, Timothy, we're going to have a talk, you and I. A long talk."

"That's fair enough," Timothy said. "That's what I want to do. Talk." She thought he smiled then, but with the fog between them, she wasn't certain.

She put the mirror down.

Chapter

11

"We?" Phoebe asked, catching Agnes's use of the word *you* in her last statement.

Agnes looked at her with those strange pale eyes. "I'm afraid I can't take any part in the struggle to come," she said. "I have nothing left to offer in the way of power, certainly not anything that begins to approach what the Charmed Ones can do and no further information that could possibly be of any use. Now, I'm sorry, but I simply must return to where I belong."

Phoebe thought she saw Agnes flicker, like a projected movie image slightly out of sync. Agnes seemed to feel it too; her gaze locked on Leo's as her eyes widened, and a shadow of terror crossed her face. "Now, Leo," she said, her tone insistent.

"Very well," Leo said. Agnes shimmered briefly and was gone, leaving behind only the faintest scent of apples. Leo shrugged, palms up.

"I'm surprised she gave us that much," he said quietly. "I guess we couldn't expect any more."

"Oh, yeah!" Phoebe exclaimed.

"What?" Piper asked, arching one eyebrow at her sister.

"We forgot to ask her about the letter," Phoebe said.

Piper shook her head sadly. "Still with the letter? Me, I'm thinking the letter is a great, big fat phony, as was the vision slash dream or whatever it was that sent you to it. Both provided by Timothy McBride, I would guess. Along with whatever spell is making us so argumentative with each other."

"But for what purpose?"

"We probably won't know that until we talk to Paige," Leo said. "But since Paige isn't here, and neither is Agnes's mirror, the logical assumption would be that Timothy wanted somehow to isolate Paige from the two of you so he could persuade her to release him from the mirror."

"I'm still a little confused about that whole deal too," Phoebe said. "How did Timothy come back if he was trapped in the mirror? And why now?"

Cole touched her shoulder gently. "I don't think we can know those answers either until we find him," he said. "But since we're all just guessing, I'd say that maybe the water flooding into his old graveyard, where he had buried the bodies that gave him his power in the first place—breaking through the floor, opening them up to the air—maybe that started the process. Gave him some kind of focus. Not enough, if Agnes is right about the mirror, to resume his full physical form. But enough to manifest some kind of presence."

"And to start killing again," Piper said. "Let's not forget that."

"Right," Cole replied. "And as we know, each murder he commits increases his power. So maybe he was able to reach a certain point, some level of manifestation, but beyond that point he knew he'd need to be released from the mirror."

"And he used me to drive a wedge in the family," Phoebe said, the full impact of what she had done hitting her suddenly, like a physical blow. She started flipping through the *Book of Shadows* again, intent on finding a spell that would neutralize whatever enchantment had been placed on them. "To make it so Paige wouldn't trust us, so she could be manipulated into doing whatever it is he needs of her."

"Which could also mean that she's in danger," Piper observed.

"And if he regains his physical form, so is just about everybody else," Leo added. "We know he's evil. Once he's whole, he can speed up the killings, taking more and more victims and gaining more and more power. He probably thinks that the last time he was here, he moved too slowly, giving your ancestors a chance to catch on. This time he's probably unlikely to make that mistake again. If he gets to be strong enough—especially if he does anything to Paige, eliminating the threat of the Power of Three—he'd be nearly unstoppable."

Until Leo said it, Phoebe had been thinking only of herself, of what she had done to the family by distrusting Paige and fighting with Piper. Now she realized that it could all be so much worse, that Timothy could be intending to hurt Paige, even to kill her. Or might already have done so. The pain she had felt a moment ago returned, tripled. Had she set her own sister up to be murdered? She blinked back hot tears. "We've got to find her, Leo. Find Paige. Now."

He was standing still, eyes closed, head inclined slightly toward the ceiling. He looked like someone lost in thought.

"I think he's ahead of you," Cole observed.

Gotta love that Charmed One radar Leo has, Phoebe thought. *It's helped us out of jams a few times. Please don't let it fail us now.*

A moment later Leo's eyes snapped open. "I've got her," he said simply. "Let's go."

Paige kept a wary eye on Timothy as she put the looking glass on the damp leaves and backed away. He still seemed wraithlike to her, not quite substantial; she felt as if she could see the bark of the tree he stood in front of, right through his semitransparent shape. He stepped toward the clearing where she'd left the mirror but stopped at its edge as though afraid to reveal himself too completely. He kept his gaze locked on to hers, burning into her eyes as if he didn't trust her not to change her mind and snatch up the glass again. *There's no way he can reach it from there*, she thought. She didn't understand why he didn't just walk up and take it.

But what he did do surprised her even more. From his position at the tree line he reached, extending his arm toward the mirror, and when it, naturally, came up short, he stretched his arm out. But as his arm passed into the clearing and into a shaft of sunlight that tore through the fog, she could see that it was wet and reflective. Paige had to blink a couple of times to be sure of what she was really seeing. His weird, inhuman arm looked as if he had simply amassed millions of water droplets and held them together through sheer force of will, as if he were one with the fog.

She knew at that moment that she had made a terrible mistake, and there was only a split second left in which to put it right again. She tried to orb out the mirror, but Timothy reacted instantly, and the mirror was suddenly surrounded by a bluish glow that seemed to shield it from her power. Maybe she couldn't orb it, but she could still pick it up, she figured. She was about to lunge for the mirror when lights flickered about her and Leo's strong arm wrapped around her waist, restraining her.

"Paige, no!" Phoebe called, panic in her voice.

She turned to see her sisters and their guys, Piper, Phoebe, Leo, and Cole, all watching as Timothy's freakish limb snatched the mirror off the mat of wet leaves. "He's not real," Piper told her.

"Not yet anyway," Cole added.

"Which is why I was trying to grab the mirror, when you stopped me," Paige said.

Leo shrugged. "He's dangerous, Paige. He's a killer."

Across the clearing, Timothy held the mirror up in front of his face, as if admiring his own reflection. He still looked ghostly in the fog, but there was a smile of supreme satisfaction spreading across his features. "You don't believe that, do you, Paige? You know me better than that. Have I ever hurt you? Or anyone?" he said.

"Not that I've seen," Paige told him. "But I trust my sisters."

"Yeah," Phoebe said, her voice sounding a little odd. Paige glanced at her and saw that her expression matched, as if she'd swallowed something unpleasant. "Sisters stick together."

"How very sweet," Timothy replied. "I was hoping you'd be an ally, Paige. We could have been a great team, you and I. But I guess you've done enough for me already." He drew back the mirror like a baseball batter ready to swing.

"I don't think so," Piper said, casting a freezing spell at him.

For a moment Paige thought it would work. He seemed to stop in mid-motion, like a bubbly glass sculpture. But then she saw that Piper had simply frozen the action of the water droplets that had constituted his physical form—all of him, not just his arm—at that second. He gathered more, though, seemingly from the very fog around him and continued with barely a heartbeat's pause, swinging the mirror hard into the trunk of the nearest tree.

The glass shattered, shards spinning into the air and falling like silvery leaves onto the layer of matted brown ones. A ferocious burst of light—but not, Paige thought, warm yellow light; instead this light had a sick, dark quality, blasted from the bent frame of the mirror, and bathed Timothy's form in its wretched glow.

The glow faded quickly, and Timothy dropped the remains of the looking glass to the wet ground. He was changed now; his flesh had substance, elasticity, color. A faint breeze caught his hair. The folds and wrinkles of his casual clothing were from genuine fabric now, and she realized that even the rustling sound they made as he moved was different, more authentic. He was no longer a construct of the fog but had assumed a new reality.

"Congratulations, Pinocchio," Paige said.

"You're a real boy. Now what?"

"Now I *can* freeze him," Piper announced, hurling another spell at him.

But Timothy flashed a wicked grin and drew a circle in the air with one finger, a circle that glowed with a fiery light and repelled Piper's spell like a shield blocking a tossed pebble. "I don't think so, sis." He laughed, touching his own cheek with his other hand. "Hey, this feels good. Thanks again, Paige. . . . On second thought, I don't know which one of you to thank the most."

Unsure of what he meant by that or how she should take it, Paige looked at her sisters. She was about to demand an explanation when Timothy gave a little three-finger wave and blinked out of sight.

"He's gone?" Paige shrieked in anger. "Just like that?"

"He was able to block Piper's spell, just like that," Leo told her. "And Paige's attempt to orb the mirror. He's apparently pretty powerful already."

"And what was he talking about, which one of us to thank the most?" Paige went on. "I mean, I'm the one who screwed up and helped him." No one answered. "Right?"

Still no answer.

"Right?"

Phoebe wrapped her arms around herself and shivered in the cold, damp air. "Ah, Paige, you're not alone in that," she said. "But I don't want to talk about it here. Let's go home, okay?"

"Sure," Paige said. "Whatever."

Phoebe nudged Leo's arm. "Okay, Leo?"

"Sure," he echoed. And this time, catching the hint, he orbed.

Darryl had immersed himself in credit card bills, trying to find any connection that hadn't shown up in the phone records, address books, or interviews of friends and family of the victims. He'd heard about a multiple murder case back East that had been cracked when it turned out that the four victims all had taken their cars to the same tire store over a period of several months. One of the clerks at the tire shop had noted their addresses from the work orders and gone to their homes, where he killed them while they slept. There was, as far as anyone was able to determine, no actual connection to tires; the victims had been strangled, not hit with tire irons or anything. So the common thread wouldn't have been immediately obvious, but it had turned up in the comparison of past credit card receipts.

But these women might as well not even have lived in the same city. San Francisco was small in area for a major metropolis, but densely packed. Some people moved from neighborhood to neighborhood with ease, while others stayed close to their own turfs or, if they lived one place and worked another, split their time between those and in transit from one to the other. But someone who lived and worked south of Market, for instance, didn't tend to spend a lot of leisure time in the Fillmore or Cow Hollow or Presidio Heights, and vice versa.

So Darryl sat, street atlas open on his desk, looking up addresses that turned up in the purchase records. He found a couple of near misses: Julia Tilton had bought some CDs at a shop in North Beach that turned out to be two doors down from a boutique where Karen Nakamura had bought a pashmina shawl, for example. And both Gretchen Winter and Sharlene Wells had shopped at the same shoe store chain on the same day, but at different branch locations.

How does this guy choose his victims? he asked himself. *There's no physical similarity between the women. There's no real commonality to location except that they're all out by themselves on empty streets or in quiet neighborhoods.* Most serial killers, he believed, were playing out some sick psychodrama in their heads, killing the same person over and over again. But this one was breaking all the rules he had ever learned about.

"Any luck? Say yes." Darryl turned to see that Lorraine Yee had come up behind his left shoulder and stood looking down at the mass of paper on his desk.

"I wish I could," he answered glumly.

"So do I. We're working against a deadline here."

"The kind where someone else is going to die if we don't find him," Darryl said.

"That too," Lorraine replied. "But I was talking about a different kind, the kind where the feds are waiting in the wings. We don't have our guy by tomorrow morning, they're taking over the case. The commissioner has already okayed it. If there's another killing tonight, they won't even wait till morning. Next crime scene, you and I won't even be allowed inside the tape."

"You're kidding," Darryl said, outraged. But he knew she wasn't.

Her flat features confirmed it. There was no laughter in her eyes, just the sadness that had been there since the task force had been formed. Darryl didn't know her well, but he knew she took her job seriously. There were rumors that maybe she even took it too seriously, unable to divorce it from her personal life. Darryl knew she was unmarried, but then so were he and half the other cops he knew, including those who had been married before.

"This is getting to you, isn't it?" he asked sympathetically. The open bullpen wasn't the best place to discuss personal feelings, but they didn't have much choice unless they went into the task force's dedicated conference room.

"It always does," she answered. "These victims could be me, my sister, my mother, you know? Their eyes haunt me, in the pictures."

Darryl knew how she felt; he didn't even like

to go into the conference room because the women whose images were tacked to the board stared at him, challenging him, even from death, to bring some kind of justice into a world that frequently went without. But if the rumors about Lorraine were true, she took copies of the pictures home, taped them up around her apartment so that she'd be reminded of them as she made breakfast, brushed her teeth, watched TV. She couldn't escape them and didn't even try.

He knew he couldn't live that way. He wondered which of them was the better cop: he, who at least tried to maintain a professional distance, even though that distance could easily be compromised, or she, who internalized the pain of the victims, living with it until the case was closed. He thought that probably she was; she, after all, had been picked to head the task force, while he was just working it. But his sense was that he would probably last longer in the job. She would burn out or flame out sooner or later. Darryl hoped it was later, and he hoped that she survived the event, whenever it happened.

With an awful suddenness, a terrible thought struck him. He had been working this case as if the killer were merely human. But what if Leo had been right in his hunch? What if the case was connected somehow with the Tenderloin slaughterhouse and the killer was a supernatural being of some kind? Darryl knew the Charmed

Ones were on the prowl, trying in their own fashion to find an answer, just as he and the task force were. If the solution turned out to be supernatural, at least he was aware of that world, and the Halliwells would tell him when they'd solved it. At that point, as he had done so many times in the past, he would cover their tracks.

But with the feds involved, he might not be able to cover. The FBI had already taken an interest in the Halliwell sisters once. If their investigation somehow pointed to the Charmed Ones or crossed paths in any way with steps the Halliwells were taking, he'd be powerless to steer the federal investigators away.

Darryl knew that the police fulfilled a necessary job in society, working to keep order and enforce the laws of the land. But the Charmed Ones performed a similar job on a much greater scale; they, and they alone, could stand as the thin line between Good and Evil in the capitalized letter sense. Their mission couldn't be compromised.

He realized that Lorraine was still standing at his shoulder, as if waiting for something. "We can't let them take the case," he said.

"You're telling me," she said. She squeezed his shoulder in an oddly familiar way, considering he didn't really know her that well. But it was, he understood, just the camaraderie of the job showing itself. They both wore the badge, and that made them close in a way that civilians could never know. "That's why we need a break. And fast."

He couldn't argue with that.

Chapter

12

All in all, Teresa Pineda thought as she carried most of a table's worth of dishes toward the kitchen, her first day on the job hadn't gone so bad. She had waitressed before, of course, so that part came easy to her. Keep a smile on your face, flirt a little, laugh a lot, don't forget the orders and don't drop anything—those were the keys. The hard part was the sheer physical exertion involved, which people who had never served food tended to underestimate. She had been on her feet for eight hours, walking fast, scooting around tables, dodging chairs when diners suddenly got to their feet without looking around first, carrying heavy trays laden with food and drink and then clearing tables after meals. Her shoes were still new and a little tight, and she'd spilled a few drops of mayo or something on them, which would clean up, she figured. The uniform was a little goofy-looking, but it fitted her well. So not that much to complain about. But she knew she'd be sore tomorrow, because she had worked muscles that hadn't been pushed so hard in some time.

Then there were the tips. She had worked in a variety of places, but never a restaurant that was as tourist-heavy as this one, right on Fisherman's Wharf. The place was decorated in someone's extreme impression of the archetypal seafood house, with nets and tridents and phony fish mounted on the walls and even nautical charts inlaid into the tables. Every business around here was geared to the tourist trade: souvenir shops, the Ripley's museum and the wax museum, the tour boats and the restored historical ships, the themed restaurants that specialized in moving large crowds through the doors in a hurry. People came in just happy to get off their feet, take the cameras off their necks, and set their shopping bags down for a while.

Teresa had turned on the charm, touched the men on their shoulders or backs, complimented the women on their clothes or their purchases, teased the kids. She had found that tips were best in neighborhood restaurants patronized primarily by local regulars, who knew they'd be coming back time and again, and had been a little worried that tourists would be lousy tippers, feeling as if they'd been spending money all day and knowing they'd never see the waitress after they walked out the door. But she had worked them, and they'd responded, and the restaurant's fast turnover played to her advantage as well. It was a tiring day, but she'd netted a couple of hundred bucks in tips, even after sharing with the hostess and the bus staff. It beat the minimum wage paycheck she had earned at the copy shop she had been working at, that was for sure. At this rate she'd not only be able to afford after-school day care for Jacky, but an occasional special treat besides. He'd been talking about wanting a Game Boy for his birthday, and she just might be able to make that happen. Plus she could replace the bracelet she'd lost somewhere.

She put her dishes on the table next to Oscar. "*Gracias,*" he said, laughing. "I was afraid I was actually going to finish."

"It's never-ending, isn't it?" she asked.

"Seems like." His hands were underwater, invisible from the forearms down. His apron looked like a modern art project, and a hairnet held back his thick mop of black curls. Like everyone else on the Sea King staff, he smelled like fish. "You're off, right?"

"Yeah, just about." Everyone worked breakfast and lunch shifts before graduating to dinners, when things, she had been warned, got really hairy.

"Doing anything special tonight?" he wanted to know.

"Picking up my kid from school. Then a long,

hot bath sounds good. Maybe sleeping for about fourteen hours."

"I hear you," Oscar said with a sympathetic grin. He brought his hands out of the dishwater to set some dishes in the next sink for rinsing, and to pull some more dirty ones in. "You did good, though, right?"

"I didn't dump soup on anybody," Teresa replied. "I hardly got anybody's order wrong, and I only lost my patience with one guy who tried to grab me the wrong way."

"So he deserved it."

"His wife thought so too." She laughed at the memory of the man's red face when she had caught his hand snaking around behind her and the way his wife had been haranguing him about it even as they left.

"And you made some bank."

She touched the pocket she'd been tucking tips into all night, feeling the comfortable roll there. "I did okay," she said. "Not bad for the first day."

"I'm glad to hear it," he told her. "I think maybe you'll work out good, be around for a long time."

Hearing him say that made a warm feeling rise in her. She thought she had done a fine job, but it was still good to have it confirmed by an independent source, someone who had no reason to lie to her. She got a comfortable vibe from the whole staff; even though they all were rushed and busy, she thought almost everyone genuinely liked the others and was happy working there.

She believed she would like this place. And if it helped her provide for Jacky, so much the better.

She tapped Oscar on the arm. "I'm going to head out then, Oscar. See you later."

"I'll see you," he replied. She headed for the tiny employee lounge to wash up, put on a sweater, and grab her purse. Jacky would be anxious for her to pick him up from day care, and she didn't want to be late.

"Okay," Paige said, pacing around the manor's living room, fists clenched at her hips. "Does somebody want to tell me what that was about? Because I kind of feel like I just walked into a movie an hour after it started and didn't even see what it was called, and I'm thinking you people know just a little bit more about it than I do."

Phoebe knew it was up to her to make things right, to try to explain what had happened, even though it would also mean exposing to Paige that she had failed to trust her. There was every chance Paige already knew that, though, if she had really gone into Phoebe's nightstand and seen the letter. Phoebe squirmed in her chair and looked to Piper for support, but all she got in return was a raised eyebrow that meant, "You're on your own, kid." Piper had refereed plenty of fights between her and Prue, so she figured it was only fair that Phoebe work this one out herself. Even if it had been a pretty one-sided fight—all hers.

"I am so sorry, Paige," Phoebe said, feeling that it would be good to start off with what would no doubt become a common theme over the next few minutes. She folded her hands in her lap and tried to look as honestly remorseful as she felt.

"Sorry for what?" Paige asked.

"I—I had this vision," Phoebe told her. She wished there were time to build a fire in the fireplace or that she could use Piper's powers to speed up the metabolism of some logs to make one, to help dispel the chill that seemed to grip her from the inside out. "A kind of dream vision. I mean, I was asleep, but it woke me up. And it was terrifying, like a nightmare."

"About me?" Paige queried sharply. "Or what?"

"Just let me do this," Phoebe snapped. "I mean—I'm sorry. This is just hard for me, Paige."

Paige shrugged and gave her a "whatever" look.

"The vision was of something important, up in the attic, inside an old dresser. I went up there, and with Cole's help I found it. It was a letter, from our Great-Great-Great-some-number-of-greats-that-I've-forgotten-Aunt Agnes. It said—"

"I know what it said," Paige interrupted.

"You read it?"

"You're not the only one who sucks," Paige said. "But you do your confession, and we'll get to mine later."

"Not much later," Leo said hopefully. "He's still out there."

Phoebe turned to him. "We have to do this, Leo. We'll have to work together if we're going to defeat him, and we can't do that until we clear the air."

"I'm just saying"—Leo was using his calm-down voice, which Phoebe knew well— "a little shorthand wouldn't hurt."

Ignoring him, Phoebe turned back to Paige. "So you know what the letter said. And you know it didn't name any sibling in particular, but the circumstances could easily have described the way you came into the family. I wouldn't have paid it any attention if I hadn't first been told about it in a vision. Those usually don't lie."

"If I can point something out, Phoebe," Cole said tentatively.

"As long as you're fast," Phoebe said. "You heard Leo."

"You weren't sure if it was a dream or a vision or some combination. Given what we know about Timothy now, I would say it was probably a dream. He was probably powerful enough, even then, to plant a dream; you yourself said once that it's not that hard to do."

"But he'd have had to get in the house to do it," Piper said.

"He's, like, fogboy," Paige said. "Or he was anyway. I think he could be anywhere the fog was, and if a little intelligent fog could sneak in the house, that'd be good enough for him."

"Intelligent fog," Piper echoed. "Nice concept."

"Which also would explain what you told me about, Piper, what happened when you scried for him," Phoebe blurted out. "The fog was all over the city, has been for the last few days. If he can be anywhere the fog is, maybe he was *everywhere* the fog is. So you really were finding him in all those places."

"Possible," Piper replied. "Or maybe I was just coming up blank because I didn't have anything physical to work with. But that's probably the same time that he enchanted us, causing us all to distrust one another."

"And making me trust him, even when I didn't want to!" Paige exclaimed. "Man, he's slick. In the slimy way."

"Anyway," Phoebe said, clasping her hands together and turning back to Paige once again, "I didn't want not to trust you. But the dream or whatever seemed so real and so urgent, and then the letter—I just didn't feel like I could take a chance. I wanted to find out more about Aunt Agnes and the whole situation."

"I tried to tell her," Piper put in.

"Yes, she did. That's true. Piper never lost faith in you for a second. And I'm so ashamed that I did I can't even tell you. So I put the letter in my room, and then—" Her expression darkened. "You were in my room, weren't you?"

Paige tried a weak smile. "I told you we both suck."

"But, Paige, that's—"

"You didn't trust me." Paige reminded her gently, touching her heart. "Your own flesh and blood."

"Could I maybe speed this up just a little?" Leo asked. "Paige, you shouldn't have snooped in Phoebe's room even though, I'm guessing, Timothy told you to. Phoebe, you shouldn't have distrusted your sister even though you read it in a letter. But you all were acting under the influence of spells you didn't even know had been placed on you."

"How did you know Timothy told me to?"

"Elementary, my dear Watson," Leo said, holding an imaginary Holmes pipe at his jaw. "The whole reason he needed to set sister against sister was to find the mirror. Which had belonged to Aunt Agnes. So he had to get you to search through Aunt Agnes's belongings, without letting your sisters know what you were up to. He couldn't physically enter the house and take the mirror. He had to build a big enough wall between you guys that you were completely isolated from the rest of the family. It's the way he always works."

"You're right," Paige said. "That's what he was doing. I was stupid not to see it at the time. But he was so nice and charming. Or at least I thought he was, before I learned that he's nothing but a big creep."

"And a mass murderer," Cole added. "Let's not lose sight of that."

"How many people has he killed?" Paige demanded.

"Lots," Leo said. "We don't have a firm count yet, but more than fifty. And he's still at it. Which is why we need to find him now. Before he does it again."

"Oh," Paige said, the blush on her cheeks vanishing as the reality sank in. "Ohhh."

"Paige, you didn't . . ." Phoebe left the thought unfinished, the mental image too awful to hold in her mind.

But Paige picked up on it. "No!" she said forcefully. "But I thought about it."

"Can I just say 'eeeeww' and second Leo's statement?" Piper put in. "I don't even want to think about that. I just want to get this bozo."

"She's right," Leo said. "Or I'm right. Let's finish this later and take care of business now."

"You are right, Leo," Paige told him. "Phoebe, he's right. I'm sorry, you're sorry, let's just be sisters and kick Timothy's butt together, okay?"

She held out a hand to Phoebe, who took it and gave it a sisterly squeeze.

"Okay," Phoebe said. "Counterspell first, and then look out, jerk. Here comes the Power of Three."

Darryl Morris and Lorraine Yee walked out of the station into the street together. The rest of the cops on the task force were already out there somewhere, tugging on their individual threads and hoping they all led to some kind of conclusion. The more Darryl looked at the case, the more he was afraid they wouldn't, that they didn't have the right threads yet. All they had were loose ends, but there was nothing in the center holding them together.

Lorraine looked up at the sky. "Getting dark."

"It's hard to tell through the fog," Darryl said. "But yeah, it looks that way."

"I kept hoping it wouldn't. That something would happen to the earth's rotation, and it would just stay daylight until I was ready for night."

"Because that's our guy's favorite time to strike." It wasn't a question. Lorraine nodded anyway.

"Not that he's unwilling to move at different times," she replied. "But yes, he likes it best in the evening. The time when most people are home from work, settled in, and the partyers are where they're going but not leaving yet. Streets are as empty as they get, but there's always someone coming or going he can home in on."

"All over the city," Darryl commented, "and somehow, he's always right there to find them."

He and Lorraine didn't have much of a plan, he knew. They were going to get into her unmarked car and drive, looking for quiet neighborhoods, hoping against hope that they could spot his victim before he did. The rest of the task force would do the same, and uniformed patrols all over the city had been told what to watch for.

With no leads, no real clues, there was nothing else they could do.

Before they'd left the building, he'd been handed a manila folder. Inside was a forensics report on the bodies found in the Tenderloin, at the former Gates Mansion. He had skimmed it quickly because Lorraine had been waiting, arms folded, tapping her fingers, impatient to get on the road.

But what he saw in the report turned his blood to ice, and he didn't know how to tell Lorraine about it. Or even if he dared.

She climbed in behind the wheel of her plain green sedan and started the engine, and they were quiet as she pulled out into the traffic. They both mentally tuned out the sounds of the police radio, as every cop learned to do, and drove a few minutes without talking, each scanning one side of the street, knowing that everyone they looked

at could be either a possible victim or a killer. *No
one knows what evil lurks,* Darryl thought. *There is
no Shadow who can read people's hearts.*

"I try to become him," Lorraine said, breaking the silence after a few blocks. The sound of
her voice in the quiet car startled Darryl.

"Who?"

"The killer. Our guy. I try to empty my mind
and think like him, feel like he does, react like he
would. So I can try to figure out what he's going
to do next, even before he knows."

"Does it work?" he asked.

"Sometimes. I've collared a few like that. The
guy they called the Butcher because he used the
big cleaver? That's how I got him."

"Doesn't it make you feel . . . I don't know,
unclean?"

Lorraine laughed, a sound that was curiously
devoid of humor. "I take a lot of showers. A *lot* of
showers. Long, hot ones. They don't help. There
are people I can talk to, you know? That doesn't
really help either, but it makes the brass happy.
Then I visit the graves of the people he killed, or
I look at the pictures of the victims, and I look at
the people on the streets that he didn't get a
chance to kill. That makes me feel better. That's
the only thing that ever really makes me feel
better."

"What about now?" Darryl asked. "When
you haven't got him yet, knowing he's still out
there."

"Then nothing works," Lorraine told him. "I still do it all, the showers, the talking, but it doesn't help. I just hurt until I get him."

"That sounds tough."

"It is. But it works sometimes, so it's worth it."

"And right now?" Darryl pressed her. "What do you feel? Where is he? What's he thinking about?"

Lorraine made a left turn onto Filbert Street. "I'm having such a hard time reading this one," she said. "He's not like the others. I can't pin him down, can't get a clear picture of him in my head."

That would make sense, Darryl knew, if Leo and the Halliwells were right about him. He would be beyond even Lorraine's vast experience.

"I know what I think." She went on. "I think he likes it. I think he's not one of those guys who try to talk themselves out of it or try to convince themselves that it's someone else doing it. This one enjoys what he's doing. He's creative. We still don't know what weapon he uses, which means it's nothing ordinary. He stabs them so many times because he gets a visceral pleasure from the act. But that all makes it harder for me to understand him, to let him inside my brain, because he's just so alien."

"I'm pretty sure you're right about that," Darryl said.

She acted as if she hadn't heard him, almost as if she were in a trance. "He likes the fog," she said. "Because the fog gives him cover, dampens the sound of his footsteps. He can sneak through it, come up out of it before she even knows he's there. She has no chance to run, to scream, before he's on her."

As she spoke—without a pause, almost as if she weren't even doing the driving—she made a sudden, screeching right onto Stockton, heading toward the water.

"Where are you going?" Darryl asked her.

"Fog's lifting a little," Lorraine explained, ticking her head toward the sky outside the windows. "It'll stay thickest close to the water. That's where he is."

Darryl didn't know if she was right about that, but it was as good a theory as any other. He shut up and let her drive.

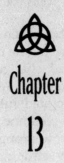

Chapter

13

Counterspell completed, Piper led the way up to the manor's attic, where she hoped to scry, once again, for Timothy McBride. She knew quite a bit more about him this time, and that might help. And Paige had salvaged the broken mirror, which he had touched, at least back when he'd been made of water instead of flesh and blood. She hoped that would be sufficient. Scrying was harder than it looked, and it could be incredibly frustrating when it didn't work. Or like the last time, when it had seemed to indicate that the object sought was everywhere at once, just as good as nowhere when it you came right down to it.

She looked at the map and the mirror, looked at her sisters, both of whom had been hurt more by this guy than she had, or at least more obviously injured. Piper liked to be the levelheaded eldest these days, but when her sisters were in pain, so was she. Even if he'd gotten to her only secondhand, he had still gotten to her; there could be no denying that. And he was still out there, as Leo had pointed out, incessantly, really, and would likely continue to kill and grow stronger, kill and grow stronger.

Who knew how strong he might become, given time enough and a city full of potential victims?

She didn't even want to think about that, didn't want to give voice to a question that could only have a terrible answer. Instead she stood before the map and raised the crystal.

Teresa Pineda had married Greg Logan when both were just twenty years old, even though most of her friends had told her she was loco. He was an Anglo, a surfer even, they said, and he wouldn't understand her way of life. He could barely speak enough Spanish to order a taco from a fast-food joint. And they were so young, crazy in love, everybody knew, but still really just kids. She had listened to all the arguments, all the rational reasons, and then they had married anyway, running off to Carson City to do it one night, almost daring each other to go through with it.

They had gone through with it. Then they came back to the city, waited for her parents to wake up in the morning and told them, and afterward drove to where his parents lived in Burlingame and told them as well. Their families seemed put out by the way that it happened, but they had known that there had been discussion of marriage, and her parents loved Greg. His parents were maybe a little afraid of Teresa, they thought she was a bit wild for their son, but they still accepted her and came to love her.

That part taken care of, they had found an apartment at the edge of the Fillmore District, where it blended into Japantown, a neighborhood where neither of them had ever lived or even spent much time. But it was cheap, and they were young and poor. Three years later, after Jacky was born, they'd moved to a bigger place, a three-bedroom apartment in North Beach. It was still a low-rent building, but with enough space for Jacky to have his own room instead of having to sleep in a crib squeezed in between their bed and a wall.

Another four years passed. Greg quit surfing, at least as often as he once had, trading in his trunks for a suit and tie and a job at a brokerage house on Sansome Street, off Market. Teresa worked a succession of part-time jobs so she could stay home with Jacky as much as possible, at least until he started school. Greg put in long hours, though, and it looked as if he were going to climb the corporate ladder quickly. One morning he was told at work that he was getting a much sought-after promotion, and that afternoon he was told at his doctor's office that he had inoperable throat cancer.

He quit the brokerage job and spent the next seven months with Teresa and Jacky and out on his surfboard. Teresa wasn't happy about the loss of income, particularly at the same time as his medical bills were piling up. But she couldn't begrudge him spending his last days doing what he truly loved. He caught his last wave three days before he died, in bed, Teresa sitting in a chair beside him reading a fat Latin American novel about love and loss. She never finished the book, but she kept it on a table in the room that had been Greg's den, where his surfboard still stood against one corner.

Now Jacky was eight, in the third grade. And money was still tight. But as she walked toward home, she allowed herself to fantasize about what two hundred dollars a day, five days a week—and then some, when her actual biweekly paycheck came in—could buy. She might even be able to pay off some of the credit card debt that had built up since Greg's insurance money had run out.

She didn't live too far from the wharf, but she had to detour three blocks out of her way in order to swing by Jacky's elementary school, where he and a few other kids of working parents waited in after-school day care that went until six thirty. She was close to the limit, she knew. The sky was getting dark overhead, and if she pushed it past the cutoff time, the center would start to charge by the minute instead of the hour. Two hundred bucks was good money, but not if she had to pay it all out for day care. She stepped up her pace a little bit.

That was when she heard the man in the fog.

Lorraine Yee drove like a crazy person, Darryl thought. She barely slowed for intersections, and she swerved around cars moving too slowly for her, whether heading uphill or down or even on blind curves. She leaned on the horn but refused to turn on her lights or siren, not wanting to alert the killer, if he was in fact out here somewhere. Her knuckles were white against the wheel, and she wrenched it from side to side as if it were a great weight, as if only her inability to muscle the car as precisely as she would have liked were preventing her from finding the killer they both wanted to catch.

"Are you sure you know where you're going?" he asked finally, after she had made a complete circuit of one block and started down the same street again.

She glanced at him, lips pulling back to bare teeth in an expression that was more of a snarl than a smile. "Of course not," she answered honestly. "I'm just trying to feel him. I think he's near the water, near the Wharf, staying where the fog is thickest. But not right at the wharf. It's way too crowded there. He'd never strike in a

busy tourist area like that. He'll be on one of the
quieter streets away from there, waiting for
someone to wander along. Someone female,
alone, most likely not even worrying about what
might be waiting for her in the fog."

"You're probably right," Darryl said. He didn't
bother to add that he thought she was going
about it in the wrong way, though, driving aim-
lessly, covering the same ground over and over
again. He had suggested they make a mental
grid out of the streets and cover them in a more
orderly fashion, east to west and then north to
south, starting at the water's edge and working
inland. But it was her car, her task force, and she
was the one trying to live inside the killer's
head. He had never been able to get so much as a
brain wave off this guy, much less the kind of
lock on him that Lorraine seemed to have. She
wanted to work from her gut, so he kept his
mouth closed and looked out the windows at the
darkening streets, searching for anyone walking
by himself, for man or woman. Trying in vain to
see what evil lurked.

More and more, as he sat helplessly in the
shotgun seat of Lorraine's car, he found himself
hoping that the Charmed Ones were out there
somewhere, closing in on the killer. Because
more and more, as he ran over the facts in his
head, he reached the same conclusion: Their
killer wasn't human. Their killer had been active
almost a hundred years ago, and he'd gone

away for a long time, but now he had come back and started up his old hobby again.

The coroner's report that he had hastily flipped through contained one pertinent piece of information that jumped out at him. The stab wounds in the Gates Mansion bodies had been made by a bayonet, of late nineteenth-century vintage. Probably a Civil War relic, Sweeney, the coroner, guessed, but that was pure speculation, not any kind of certainty. By the same token, Sweeney couldn't determine whether the bayonet had been mounted on a rifle or loose. He assumed that it had been handheld, though, on the basis of the angle of some of the stab wounds.

He had included some pictures and a couple of drawings to demonstrate what he thought the wounds would have looked like when they were fresh and maybe what the weapon would have looked like. He had even made a note in the margin of one of his sketches. "Looks kind of like the work of your wet killer," he had written.

Darryl knew that he was right. The stab wounds the wet killer left behind, by a weapon they could not identify, had the same kind of triangular character as the wounds that Sweeney had drawn. They weren't absolutely identical, and anyway, Darryl knew that if the killer were using an antique bayonet, it would leave traces behind, bits of rust, flecks of metal, but they were very, very close.

Close enough to make him think that these murders were committed by the same person. Or whatever he was.

Close enough to make him hope the Charmed Ones were nearby.

"Fisherman's Wharf," Piper announced.

"He's eating seafood?" Paige asked.

"The waitress!" Phoebe almost shrieked, remembering her vision of the woman with the sauce on her shoes and a fishy smell. "In the seafood restaurant uniform. She could easily be from one of the restaurants down there."

"He's not exactly at the wharf," Piper said. "A few blocks away. Near Leavenworth and Chestnut. Leo?"

"Your chariot awaits, madam," Leo said. He took Piper's arm in his and orbed them all to the corner she had mentioned.

But the corner was deserted.

"Piper," Phoebe growled, her tone accusatory, "you said—"

"I know," Piper said, waving her hands to try to keep Phoebe's voice down. "I just said what I scried. I still think he's around here somewhere."

"He's not fogboy anymore," Paige said, "so he should be easier to spot."

"But the fog's still pretty dense here," Cole observed. "Even for real people. You can't see to the end of the block."

"So which way?" Phoebe asked. "Do we just start calling for seafood lady?"

"And tip him off?" Paige replied. "I don't want to give him a chance to hide from us. I want to get him."

"Here's a clue, Paige," Phoebe said. "The hiding thing? I think he's already got that going on."

"Let's split up," Piper said. She pointed up Leavenworth. "I'll go this way. Paige, you go down the block there. Phebes, take Chestnut." She pointed again, west down Chestnut Street. "And, Cole, you go the other way."

"What about me?" Leo asked.

"Stay here and back up whoever yells first," Piper instructed him.

Leo nodded, and they all had taken their first hesitant steps into the thick fog when they heard the silence-shattering scream, emanating from somewhere up Leavenworth.

"Or we all could just go there!" Paige shouted, spinning on her heel and starting up the block.

Piper was already moving in that direction, Phoebe knew. Though she had taken off on the side street, she also knew that her sisters would need her, that the three of them were going to have to work together if they were going to beat this foe. He'd nearly conquered by dividing once. She wasn't about to let him do it again.

• • •

Teresa had noticed the scuffing sound of a shoe on pavement as soon as she had changed the pace of her own steps, speeding up to beat the deadline for picking up Jacky. It was as if someone had been matching her, step for step, and her altered speed had thrown the person off. She came to a sudden halt and peered into the fog, trying to see if there was really anyone around or if it was simply her imagination, kicked into overdrive by the unfamiliar, if not unpleasant, sensation of cash in her pocket.

It would really stink big time to be robbed today, she thought. Also, she'd noticed something in the headlines this morning on her way to work, about a killer in the city. But she hadn't had time to stop for a paper, so she didn't know what that was all about. Anyway, she saw no one, so she continued, redoubling her speed to make it to Jacky's school before six thirty.

It was then, as she sped up her pace dramatically, that the other figure started to run. Giving up any pretense of stalking her, someone burst through the fog, coming straight toward her at an all-out sprint. Teresa's first impulse was to scream, and she did, drawing a big breath of air into her lungs and then expelling it as loudly and ear-piercingly as she could manage. If, for some reason, the guy coming toward her was just a jogger who'd lost his way in the fog or had some other innocent excuse for startling her, then she would be embarrassed. But if he had

mischief on his mind, she had put him on notice
and called for help. Anyway, he didn't look like
a jogger—he wore a T-shirt and jeans, with
heavy boots, and he had a vicious, menacing
grin fixed on his face.

He kept coming, though, ignoring her scream.
As he neared, Teresa noticed something else: At
first, his hand was empty, but as he approached
her, he seemed to scoop fog from the very air,
somehow shaping it into a long, pointed
weapon.

Teresa screamed again at the sight of that, it
was so odd that she thought she must have misunderstood what she'd seen, since it was clearly
impossible. But there was no answer to her
screams, and she believed they must have gone
unheard or been ignored. She looked about des-
perately for an escape route, someplace to hide.
A metal garbage can, overflowing with refuse,
stood near the edge of the sidewalk, and she
snatched up the round lid and threw it, discus-
style, at the guy, who was still coming toward
her. He swatted it away without even pausing.
She kicked the whole can toward him, sending
the scents of rotting fruit and stale beer spraying
into the night, and it rolled into his path. As he
tried to step over it, the toe of one of his heavy
boots skidded across the rolling barrier, and he
tumbled headlong to the sidewalk, slamming
down hard. When he hit, his weird dagger dissipated into fog and drifted off with the evening

mist. But an instant later there was another one in its place.

Teresa turned and ran again, intent on taking full advantage of his momentary delay. But he too was up in no time, and before she'd put a dozen steps between them, he had closed the gap. She felt the impact of a solid fist against her shoulder, spinning her around, and she careered into the side of the nearest brownstone building. The rough surface ripped at her cheek. She tasted blood inside her mouth, saw stars, turned herself around again, and shoved herself away from the wall—right into his waiting arms, powerful and fierce.

Lorraine Yee had been right. The fog, dissipating throughout most of the city, remained thick near the waterfront. Driving through it was, Darryl thought, like flying through clouds or maybe the thick smoke of a bad fire. He tried to see through it, but visibility was limited to a couple of blocks at the most, and sometimes far less. As they crossed Leavenworth, Darryl, subtly gripping the edges of his seat so Lorraine wouldn't notice how hard he was trying to keep his head from bouncing off the car's ceiling any more than it already had, could barely see from one side of the street to the other.

What fog did to visibility, he knew, it also did to sound, in a lesser way. Fog or low clouds dampened sound, kept it from traveling as far as it otherwise might. On quiet city streets, where a scream of terror could otherwise echo for blocks and blocks, fog might eliminate some of the echo, keeping the sound confined to a much smaller area and maybe even changing the pitch.

Making it sound, in other words, sort of like the noise that Darryl thought he had just heard. He squinted and looked down the block. Were those figures he saw, moving through the mist? There was no way to tell, and before he could even tell Lorraine to stop, they had bounced through that intersection and were rocketing toward the next one.

"I thought I heard something," he told her.

"Heard what?"

"I don't know. But it could have been a scream."

She glanced at him. "You want me to turn around?"

He considered it briefly. They were on Greenwich, heading toward Hyde. Hyde was one-way so they couldn't safely hang a right there, and even if they could, they couldn't double back on Lombard. The block that had earned it the sobriquet "The Crookedest Street in the World" ran between Hyde and Leavenworth, and even if it wasn't backed up with tourist traffic, trying to take that hill with its series of sharp hairpins would slow them down more than just bypassing Hyde and Lombard, going to Larkin and cutting back down Chestnut. The only thing that might delay them was running into cable car traffic on Hyde.

He looked around to see if it was safe for Lorraine to pull a screaming U-turn in the middle of the block. A few cars rushed by in each direction, and he decided it wasn't safe. Circling to Chestnut would cost a couple of minutes, but since they were almost to Hyde, it was still the quickest way back to where he had heard the maybe scream.

Or it could have been a cat screeching, or some kids playing, or a TV set turned too loud. There was just no way to tell without checking it out.

"No," he finally answered. "Larkin to Chestnut, then back to Leavenworth."

"Got it," Lorraine answered, tight-lipped. She sped through the intersection with Hyde, foot heavy on the gas. At Larkin, she leaned into the right turn.

As soon as Paige broke through the thickest part of the fogbank, she was able to recognize Timothy. He'd changed his clothes, replacing the casually dressy ones he'd worn for her with more practical attire, practical, at least, for the murderous thug she now knew he was. In one hand he wielded a strange, long knife with three sharp edges in a T shape. Timothy was still substantial, she thought, but the knife looked like a fog weapon, the way his arm had been back in the park.

In his other hand was a young woman who must have been the waitress Phoebe had described, the one from her vision. *So we're here in time to save the innocent*, she thought. *I hope.* She, Piper, and Phoebe all ringed Timothy, with Leo and Cole at their backs.

"Timothy!" She screamed his name, and glancing back over his shoulder toward her, he tossed her a vicious grin. She knew he could just shimmer away again, if he chose to, though they were prepared to try to stop him. But it seemed he wanted to wrap up what he was doing first.

"I'll be right with you, Paige." He drew back the wicked knife, readying it for what looked like a stab to the heart. "Just let me finish up here."

But his intended victim was anything but compliant. When he turned to look at Paige, she curled her fingers into a claw and raked it across his face. Timothy let out a yowl of pain that did Paige's heart good.

"That hurt!" he snarled.

"Not used to a little pain?" Paige asked. "You'd better *get* used to it. It's part of life in the real world you're so anxious to rejoin."

"I'd rather be used to inflicting it," Timothy replied. "But once I've rid the world of this clawing cat I'll happily practice on you."

"I hate to shatter your illusions, Timmy," Paige said, diminishing his name with the best sneer she could muster, "but that's just not going to happen."

He ignored her taunting and began his forward thrust, the one that would finally impale the waitress, who still struggled in his grasp. Paige didn't think she could orb the fog knife, which was as much a part of him as his own fingers, but she was faster than his knife strike, and she orbed him away from the woman, making him reappear about eight feet off the sidewalk. Startled, he drove the knife forward into thin air. He tried to turn again, to glare at Paige and her sisters, but Piper froze him in that awkward instant, feet scrabbling for purchase, shoulders hunched, neck twisted, a furious scowl marring his otherwise handsome features.

When Paige dropped him back to the sidewalk, he bounced a little but held his position, stiff as a statue.

"Careful," Piper said. "You might break him."

"Wouldn't that be a crying shame?" Phoebe asked teasingly. She was already at work laying out the vanquishing stones, forming a kind of half circle around Timothy's rigid form. The waitress, Paige noticed, watched the proceedings in stunned fascination.

"You might want to get out of here," Paige told her. "Like, in a hurry. Before you see something you really don't want to see."

"Been there, done that," the waitress replied, still trying to catch her breath from the experience. "But thanks. Thanks a lot. I really mean that."

Paige brushed away her gratitude with a wave of her hand. *All in a day's work*, she thought. She was glad they'd saved the woman's life, but at this moment finishing Timothy once and for all was her priority. When she looked up again, the waitress had taken her advice and was already turning a corner, heading out of sight.

Paige looked at her sisters, Piper, gaze fixed on Timothy, making sure he couldn't somehow use his powers to break free of her freezing spell, and Phoebe, finished setting the stones and looking on with her hands on her hips, a familiar, comfortable smile playing across her face. Behind them, keeping out of the fight and letting the sisters handle things, the men her sisters loved looked on.

"All at once?" Phoebe asked. "Or should I just go for it?"

Piper raised a hand to stop her. "I think we ought to let Paige take care of this one."

Phoebe glanced at her and nodded. "I think you're right. Sis? The honor is all yours."

Paige allowed her own gaze to return to Timothy once more. She felt ashamed of how she'd let herself be used by him, how easily she'd fallen into his web of lies. But there was one sure cure for that shame, and the time had come to put it into play. She thought hard for a moment and came up with the words she wanted to use.

The Power of Three,
Once put asunder,
Renews itself,
And sends you under.

Timothy bucked once, fear and pain etching a map of torment on his face as Piper's time freeze spell was canceled. In a moment the source of his fear and his pain became evident: a crackling sound, a biting, rancid smell, and then flames burst from underneath his skin, consuming him in a single, massive fireball.

The sisters watched, hands finding one another's, fingers twining together, until he was gone, leaving nothing but a faint scorch mark on the sidewalk. It already looked old, as if something had burned there once years before, and Paige thought that probably it would be faded completely by morning. Timothy's legacy would last awhile longer than that, she knew. The people who had loved his victims would remember their losses for their lifetimes. But he would take no more innocents, and in time even those who mourned would remember only happy times with their loved ones, and the cycle of the seasons would continue, birth and life and death carrying on in their eternal rhythm, and Timothy would no longer be a part of that. He would lose, as evil always lost, because even his murders would one day lose their power to cause pain.

He had already lost. He was already gone. That was good enough for now. Tomorrow would be a different day, one without Timothy McBride in it. She would go back to work, and she would figure out a way to help poor Mr. Boone, and that would bring her a different kind of satisfaction.

"You know what?" Paige said.

"What?" Piper asked.

"Let's go home. Hang out together. Watch some TV, play a game, I don't know. Whatever families do."

"That sounds good to me," Phoebe said. She snapped her fingers. "Ride, Leo?"

As he orbed them away, Leo muttered, "I always thought it was, 'Home, James.'"

Epilogue

Home it was, but only for a little while.

Shortly after they arrived, Piper happened to glance at the clock on the kitchen wall. "Yikes," she said. "It's later than I thought."

Paige felt her heart sink a little. "You working tonight, Pipe?"

"I pretty much have to," Piper replied with a little shrug. "I'm not rich enough to be one of those absentee owners, you know? They know what to do when I'm not there, but it's a lot easier on everyone if I am."

"So much for our sisterly night at home," Phoebe said with a frown.

But Paige let a slow grin cross her features. "We don't have to be at home. We can be sisterly anywhere," she said. "And sometimes it's more fun to be sisterly someplace where there's music and dancing and lots of people and noise."

Phoebe didn't even have to think about it. "I'm up," she announced. "Okay with you, Piper?"

Piper showed them both her serious face. "Hmm, let's see . . . people want to come to my nightclub and spend time. Not to mention money. People who, in addition to being my sisters, also happen to be attractive young women whose very presence there will encourage men to want to spend time, and therefore money, at my nightclub. No, I think I'd be okay with that."

"Money?" Paige asked. "You're not going to comp us?"

Piper threw up her hands in a pantomime of despair. "You drive a hard bargain. Okay, I'll comp you. But tips are out of your own pockets. And I don't want to hear about any lousy tippers."

Paige noticed Phoebe looking at the floor. "What, Phebes?"

"You know that job interview today wasn't exactly a stellar success," she said. "I don't think they're going to offer me a job. In fact, they may have to get the whole building fumigated, because I dared sneeze inside it, and I wouldn't be surprised if they sent me the bill."

"In this case, it sounds like not offering you the job would be a blessing," Cole observed.

"A job would be a good thing," Phoebe replied. "Just maybe not this one."

"I'll cover you tonight, Phoebe," Paige said. Tips wouldn't amount to that much anyway, and what was the point of putting up with Mr.

Cowan's abuse if she couldn't take her own sister out once in a while? "My treat. In fact, the
whole party's my treat." She glanced at Piper,
who gave a subtle nod. "The tips, that is, since
the rest of it is Piper's treat."

She saw Cole and Leo exchange glances. They
would come along. Cole no longer had demonic
business taking him away at night, and as long
as Leo didn't have pressing Whitelighter affairs
to manage, he liked to be where Piper was.

That was okay with her. The more the merrier
was a cliché, but sometimes it was true. She had
a feeling tonight would definitely be one of
those times.

They'd been at P3 for about an hour when
Darryl Morris showed up. His dark blue suit
was wrinkled and dirty, his cheeks were stubbled,
and all in all, Phoebe thought, he looked like a
guy who had too much irritation and not
enough sleep in his life. But he smiled as he
approached the semicircular booth where she'd
been sitting next to Paige, who chattered away
happily in that Paige-like way she had. Cole sat
on the other side of her—that she liked—and
Leo on the other side of Paige, with a space
saved at the end of the bench for Piper to use in
those few moments she could get away from her
duties and join them.

Now Leo indicated the empty space. "Take a
load off, Inspector?" he said.

Darryl nodded and sat down with a heavy sigh, putting his hands on the tabletop and lowering himself slowly onto the bench as if he carried a heavy weight on his shoulders.

"Long day?" Phoebe asked him, speaking loudly to be heard over the pounding music.

"The longest kind," Darryl replied. "And I still have to go back in and wrap up some more paperwork before I'm off."

"You're still on duty?" Cole asked. "Is this an official visit?"

"Only in the most unofficial sense," Darryl answered. He lowered his voice, so Phoebe had to lean toward him to hear. "Nobody knows I'm here. When I'm gone, even I won't remember I was ever here."

"Got it," Phoebe said.

"You do?" Paige asked. "Because I'm not sure it makes a lot of sense to me—"

"I'll explain later," Phoebe told her.

Darryl looked at everyone sitting around the half circle of table. They all waited expectantly for him to speak. "So, the strangest thing happened to me tonight," he said finally.

"What was that?" Paige asked.

"I was riding with another detective, through the foggiest part of the city, down by the water, trying to spot our killer before he took another victim."

"Did you find him?" Leo, the picture of innocence, asked.

Darryl ignored the question. "At one point I was pretty sure I heard a scream. It was a little hard to tell, though, in the moving car, with other cars around, and the fog and everything. I even thought that maybe I saw some people moving through the fog, but I couldn't be sure of that, either. So we drove around a couple of blocks and came back; this was on Leavenworth, near Chestnut. And when we came back to where I thought I had seen people, there was nobody around. We didn't hear any more screams or anything. The area was just deserted."

"Fog can be a funny thing," Phoebe said. "Tricky."

Darryl continued to ignore. "There was nobody at all around when we got there. We cruised on, and a couple of blocks up we saw a young woman, on foot, running like her life depended on it. She was wearing a waitress's uniform. Nice young lady. We stopped her and asked her where she was going in such a hurry, and she said she was late picking her son up from day care. I asked her if she had seen or heard anything strange, and she said that she hadn't, so we let her go get her boy."

"Is that unusual, Darryl?" Paige asked. "For people *not* to see strange things?"

"In this city," Darryl answered, "kind of, yes. But the point is that when you've been a cop for a long time, as I have, you can pretty much tell when someone is lying to you. And that woman was lying. No doubt about it. But since she didn't appear to have done anything wrong, I just let her go on her way. I decided that what I should do is to ask you folks if you know anything about any strange events that might have happened in that neighborhood tonight or any screams in the fog down there."

"Us?" Phoebe queried. "You want to know if we saw anything?"

Piper had approached and hovered just within earshot, and now she came closer and bent over the table.

"This is about the killer you've been after, right?" she asked Darryl. Without waiting for an answer, she went on. "I'd say the best thing for you to know is that he won't be a problem for you anymore. Or a danger to any more innocents."

"But you—"

Piper cut him off. "The murders are over. The house in the Tenderloin, with all the bodies? That killer's gone too. There won't be any trial, but just take our word for it."

"Same guy?" Darryl asked. "A hundred years later?"

"Same guy," Paige replied.

"This is one killer who's never going to bother San Francisco again," Piper announced. "Not now, not a hundred years from now. Not ever."

"Well, I'm glad to hear that," Darryl said.

"I'm not quite sure how to account for it in paperwork, but—" He stopped and smiled, as if remembering something pleasant. "But I won't have to. As of midnight tonight, this is an FBI matter. They'll be asking the questions, and if there are no answers, they're the ones who are going to have to explain why in their paperwork." He laughed and slapped the table. "I think this might be a first," he said.

"What's that?" Cole inquired.

"The first time that knowing the Halliwells has actually made my life easier." Then a dark scowl crossed his face. "You're sure about this, right? I mean, you're really sure?"

Paige was the first one who spoke up. "Sometimes you just have to trust somebody, Darryl," she told him. "I think that's all we can say. Just trust us."

The detective pushed himself out of the booth, smiling again. "Then that's what I'll do," he told them. "Thanks." He started to walk away but then stopped, leaned over the table, and looked at them, all seriousness. "I hope there's nothing out there that can connect you to any of this business," he said. "Nothing that the FBI might find."

They all considered the question for a moment, but Cole was the one who spoke up. "I don't think so," he said. "I'm pretty sure there are no tracks. And if there are, we'll just deal."

"Okay," Darryl said, nodding gravely. "You

do that." Then he turned and threaded his way out through the crowd.

When he was gone, Phoebe turned to Paige. "That was some good advice, Paige," she said. "Very smart."

"What?"

"The part about just trusting someone. I'm really going to work on that."

"Sometimes it's hard," Paige said with a giggle. "But I think it's worth a try."

Phoebe looked at her little sister, who could come across as so shallow sometimes, but who had deep wells of insight she could plumb when she needed to. Maybe growing up away from the other sisters had given her a different approach to things, a different way of looking at the world, viewing problems through a Matthews angle, instead of a Halliwell one, perhaps. Whatever it was, Phoebe was glad her sister had it, and she knew that in this case, Paige was definitely right.

Trust was always worth a try.

As many as one in three
Americans with HIV...
DO NOT KNOW IT.

More than half of those
who will get HIV this year...
ARE UNDER 25.

HIV is preventable.
You can help fight AIDS.
Get informed. Get the facts.

www.knowhivaids.org
1-866-344-KNOW

"We're the protectors of the innocent.
We're known as the Charmed Ones."

–Phoebe Halliwell, "Something Wicca This Way Comes"

Go behind the scenes of television's sexiest supernatural thriller with *The Book of Three*, the *only* fully authorized companion to the witty, witchy world of *Charmed*!

Published by Simon & Schuster

Charmed.

"We all need to believe that magic exists."
–Phoebe Halliwell, "Trial by Magic"

When Phoebe Halliwell returned to San Francisco to live with her older sisters, Prue and Piper, in Halliwell Manor, she had no idea the turn her life—*all* their lives—would take. Because when Phoebe found the Book of Shadows in the Manor's attic, she learned that she and her sisters were the Charmed Ones, the most powerful witches of all time. Battling demons, warlocks, and other black-magic baddies, Piper and Phoebe lost Prue but discovered their long-lost half-Whitelighter, half-witch sister, Paige Matthews. The Power of Three was reborn.

Look for a new Charmed novel every other month!

Published by Simon & Schuster